Other Books by Randy Jurado Ertll

Hope in Times of Darkness: A Salvadoran American Experience
Esperanza en Tiempos de Oscuridad: La Experiencia de un Salvadoreño Americano
The Life of an Activist: In The Frontlines 24/7
In The Struggle: Chronicles
The Lives and Times of El Cipitío: La Vida y los Tiempos del Cipitío
The Adventures of El Cipitío: Las aventuras del Cipitío
La Siguanaba and The Magical Loroco

Race Wars: El Cadejo

a novel by

Randy Jurado Ertll

Published in the United States of America by

ERTLL PUBLISHERS

www.randyjuradoertll.com

ISBN 978-1-7342708-4-6 (pbk.)
ISBN 978-1-7342708-5-3 (ebk.)

First edition 2020

Printed in the United States of America

1 2 3 4 5 6 7 8 9 10

Race Wars:
El Cadejo

CHAPTER 1

How can dos gemelos be of different colors? One was El Cadejo Blanco and the other one was El Cadejo Negro. He wondered, El Cadejo Blanco, why hell had chosen him to be their representative on earth. He was created by the Prince of Darkness. He had to battle his inner demons. And to make matters more complicated he had a twin to deal with, his nemesis, El Cadejo Negro.

He was conceived in *La Puerta del Diablo. The Devil's Door* that remains open in El Salvador.

At the top of La Puerta del Diablo, a cool breeze never ceases. But beneath that door, the pits of hell contain boiling volcanic lava and you can hear the screams of the fallen souls.

In 1540, El Cadejo stood atop La Puerta del Diablo en los Planes de Renderos and wondered how it would be to travel up to the northern coast on a ship. He decided that he would move to El Puerto de Acajutla and begin the building of three ships that would eventually land, in 1542, in present day San Diego, California.

Guanacos (Salvadorans) have been present in the land that is now known as the United States, since the 1500s. No joke. Who do you think brought the *Flor de Izote* plant to the United States? They came aboard the ships that they built in El Puerto de Acajutla. The ship's names were *San Salvador, San Miguel,* and *La Victoria.* Stowaways included La Siguanaba, El Duende, and El Cipitio. Rumors circulate that they landed in San Diego, migrated all the way up to San Francisco, but eventually decided to settle in present day Los Angeles, California. Rumors continue to circulate that these spirits continue to roam throughout Los Angeles and that El Cipitio is buried in the Angelus-Rosedale Cemetery.

El Conquistador Pedro de Alvarado began the expedition preparations in 1540. El Cadejo Blanco had a demonic idea, he would cast a spell on Alvarado's horse once they arrived in Mexico, so that the possessed horse would crush el pinche Conquistador to death. What an irony, Pedro de Alvarado had crushed the Pipil/Mayan resistance in Central America, but he eventually was crushed to death by his own horse in 1541.

Juan Rodriguez Cabrillo took over the expedition as its leader and was given the credit of being the first European to have explored the coast of California, hence the name of various coastal areas named Cabrillo beach.

El Cadejo Negro boarded the San Salvador ship. And El Cadejo Blanco hid within the San Miguel ship. They detested La Victoria ship since Pedro de Alvarado had named that ship after the successful conquest of the Spanish colonizers over the Mayan people of El Salvador. La Siguanaba, El Duende, and El Cipitio hid within the La Victoria ship.

El Cadejo Blanco would help to implement the colonizer plan to steal the lands from the Native Americans/indigenous.

El Cadejo Negro would have to fight the evil and wicked ways of El Cadejo Blanco who blended in well with the Spanish colonizers.

El Cadejo Blanco had already offered his expert colonization and enslavement strategies to the Portuguese and was the chief architect in stealing slaves from the São João Bautista Portuguese ship in 1619 and made a deal with the British. The 20 Angolan slaves were forcefully moved to the White Lion British ship that brought the first slaves to the East Coast of the United States. The White Lion ship landed in 1619 on Virginia state lands. Guess who was on that ship, El Cadejo Blanco!

The Spanish colonizers, Alvarado's and Cabrillo's, secret mission was to explore North America for Spain to steal more lands for the King and Queen of Spain. But the British spoiled their plans since they had already begun the plunder of North American lands before Spain.

El Cadejo Blanco became the best consultant for the Spanish empire in how to infiltrate and conquer the Mayan and Aztec empires. La Malinche actually was the owner of El Cadejo Blanco who was true guide for the Spanish colonizers when they penetrated *Tenōchtitlan*. The Aztec Empire was fully colonized by the Spanish in 1521. El Cadejo became part of the *Pipiltin* – noble social class within the Aztecs. But he betrayed them and decided to become an ally of the Spanish and even led thousands of Aztecs into present day Guatemala, Honduras, El Salvador, and other Central American countries.

The indigenous became known as Pipiles in El Salvador.

El Cadejo contributed in the destruction of their history, culture, and way of life. Their lands were viciously stolen. If they resisted, El Cadejo, along with the noble class Conquistadores and traitor mestizos were merciless in torturing and murdering the indigenous. Their temples, homes, agriculture, and books were burned. The Mayan bible, Popol Vuh, was censored and burned and the Catholic/Christian bible replaced the Popol Vuh. Made available only in Spanish language. The indigenous were forced to forget their native languages and were required to adopt the Spanish language. The official language of the land.

El Cadejo imposed Catholism and required the indigenous to convert. They had to read and follow the Christian bible. Not the Popol Vuh. The Popol Vuh included the Mayan hero twins: El Cipitio and El Duende. But this history was prohibited.

El Cipitio was made out to be a character to be feared and to scare children. Also, El Duende was used as a character to scare children and adults. The Spanish and mestizos began to tell people, "behave, read the Christian bible, or El Duende will come out of the forest and mountains to come and steal your children at night."

The Mayans were terrified of El Cipitio and El Duende. They were also taught to be frightened of La Siguanaba – the mother El Cipitio and El Duende. They described her as an evil, wicked woman who had grotesque features. She had long sagging breasts, long hair, and razor sharp nails.

El Cadejo Blanco also prohibited the Natuatl language to be spoken by the native indigenous of Central America.

The indigenous were no longer allowed to roam the land naked. They had to emulate and dress similar to the Spanish conquistadores. The priest from the missions and churches required the indigenous to dress and for women to cover their breasts.

El Cadejo Blanco began to develop a colonization master plan/strategic plan to take over the area now known as Norte America. He wanted to get paid via the strategic plan that he would submit to the Spanish king and queen to develop the establishment of the Catholic Church throughout North and South America. With a special focus on converting the indigenous to Catholicism.

El Cadejo Blanco came up with the idea: he titled his strategic plan The Virus. He would recommend to the Spanish kingdom to bring rats, mice and other animals already infected with deadly viruses. This would help to spread disease and death among the Native Americans.

El Cadejo Blanco was a psychopath with no conscience, emotions, or empathy. His number one God was gold and money.

El Cadejo Negro wanted to spread a message of hope, peace, and sharing. While he was on the San Salvador ship heading to present day San Diego, California, he began to daydream in how he would help to protect the indigenous and the natural resources of the lands that they would soon land on. He felt a strong calling and kindred. He knew that Native Americans admired wildlife and did not destroy or kill it just for fun. They hunted buffalo, dears, and other animals to eat and survive. El Cadejo Negro also knew that the Native Americans saw dogs as human's best friend. He knew that humans had migrated from Africa, to Europe, Asia, and eventually through present day Alaska to arrive in North America. The dogs were the ones that protected humans and helped them to survive by knowing where to find food, water, and safe navigation routes.

He knew that Native Americans saw black, white, and all types of colors of dogs as equal. El Cadejo Negro knew that Native Americans had foreseen the future and that the English, French, Dutch, Spanish, and other conquistadores would one day arrive to pilfer and destroy the lands.

El Cadejo Negro's mission was to warn the Native Americans that the British and Spanish settlers were coming and that they had an evil, wicked ally that could not be destroyed: El Cadejo Blanco.

He knew that El Cadejo Blanco was capable of anything to gain money and gold. He would lie, cheat, and kill. El Cadejo Negro had already witnessed the savagery and inhumanity since Cristobal Colon arrive in the Salvador Island in 1492. He saw the greed of Cristobal Colon and how El Cadejo Blanco had unleashed death, violence, and hatred withing the Carribean, Mexico, Central America, and South America.

In 1519, El Cadejo Negro tried, desperately, to prevent the invasion of Hernán Cortés and the conquest of Tenochtitlán. This is where Hernán Cortés enslaved Malintzin – who eventually became known as La Malinche. Cortés gave her the Spanish name of Marina. She was the official translator for the Spanish Conquistadores. What the history writers have left out is that La Malinche was the owner of El Cadejo Blanco. El Cadejo Blanco knew the secrets routes in how to infiltrate the Aztec Empire whose headquarters were located in Tenochtitlán. El Cadejo Blanco was the actual guide to lead the Spanish Conquistadores, with their indigenous tribe's allies, who were enemies of the Aztec Empire.

In 1520, the Mechicas actually defeated Hernán Cortés Spanish troops and his indigenous allies. It is known as the Noche Triste. Pedro de Alvarado led the charge of the troops and when Cortés arrived, he soon realized that the Mechicas had the upper hand. He tried to retreat through the darkness of night but the Mechicas attacked with no mercy. To the point that Hernán Cortés was seen crying like a baby. The Mechicas began shouting at him and calling him "pinche chillon!." He swore by a tree, while he cried, that he would return and defeat the Mechicas. He had top advisors that would help him achieve that dream of revenge: La Malinche and El Cadejo Blanco.

In 1521, Hernán Cortés, with the help of La Malinche and the expert consulting services of El Cadejo Blanco returned and led the efforts to defeat the Aztec Empire. El Cadejo Blanco purposely coughed violently on the Aztec leaders to infect them of smallpox. El Cadejo specifically coughed on Moctezuma II. Soon, millions upon millions of Aztecs and Mayans died due to the evil spread of viruses by El Cadejo Blanco. He howled with laughter and his eyes went from deep blue to blood shot red. *Rojos como brasas.*

The eyes of El Cadejo Negro were light brown and had a flicker of light and hope within them. Similar to Neil

Diamond's eyes when he sang 'Sweet Caroline.' El Cadejo's dream was to meet Neil Diamond and drink some Crackling Rosé sparkling wine. Neil's favorite. El Cadejo Negro's eyes expressed love, purity, forgiveness, and redemption. On the other hand, El Cadejo Blanco's eyes expressed hatred, betrayal, death, and fury. They reflected the pits of hell!

Once his contract with the Spanish Empire was completed, El Cadejo Blanco decided to settle in the land now known as Los Angeles, California. El Cadejo Negro decided to travel the world.

He took on the persona of William Ellis, an African American who claimed to be Mexican and went by the names of Guillermo Enrique Eliseo o Guillermo Ellis. He lived from 1864 to 1923 and became a multi millionaire who would used his skills to pass as Mexican since he had a particular fascination with Mexico since slavery did not exist there. He also heard from his family that over 4,000 black slaves fled the United States to Mexico (between 1861 to 1865), during the U.S. Civil War – to obtain their freedom. He wanted to prove to the White man, that a Black man could become a multi-millionaire. However, he had to pretend to be a Mexican – to the point that he also learned how to speak Spanish fluently.

Slavery of Africans did exist in Mexico since 1519 but after the Mexican Independence from Spain in 1821, slavery was outlawed and slaves were emancipated, especially the slaves who were 14 years old and under. El Cadejo Negro even moved to New York to establish his Wall Street import and export business of leather, cotton, and other goods. He conducted import and exports. He also took on the persona of a Cuban (Jose Marti) in New York and sometimes claimed to be Hawaiian too. Just for kicks. William Ellis goal was to pass as White or Mexican, to be able to establish colonies of Blacks in Mexico – to provide jobs for them. Once El Cadejo Negro became bored he would move on to other adventures and countries.

He even moved to Japan for a while since dogs have been respected and venerated. He even became well known and adopted an owner who named him Hachiko. The whole country became enamored with Hachiko. They even built statues to honor him and some began to pray to El Cadejo Negro. The 124th emperor of Japan, Hirohito, became intrigued by Hachiko's popularity – to the point that he was jealous.

El Cadejo Blanco heard of Hachiko, and he became envious and jealous. El Cadejo Blanco decided to visit Japan to speak to Emperor Hirohito, in order to offer his expert consulting services. Eventually, El Cadejo Blanco did end up serving as Hirohito's advisor during World War II. El Cadejo Blanco told Emperor Hirohito "you should support White Supremacy, white is might. Hitler is a loveable fella." El Cadejo Blanco was so sneaky that he carried a special potion to make Kings, Queen, presidents, and Emperors todos dundos. He would prepare a *sopa de pitos* that would make anyone sleepy and truly docile and easily fooled and persuaded. That was El Cadejo Blanco's secret recipe: una sopa de pitos. He would carry the pito plants, just in case he would meet with people that he would want to manipulate.

El Cadejo Blanco also had the power of sharing Fairy Tales that people would believe. In the 1500s, he created a rumor that California was actually an island. The dundo Europeos believed his myth making prodigiousness. He even convinced the Spanish Empire that nothing of worth was in the island of California. That they should focus on Mexico, Centroamerica, El Caribe, y Sur America.

He wanted California for himself. El Cadejo Blanco had teleporting powers and he could transport himself to any place in the world. That is why he would disappear for long periods of times since he would travel and offer his consulting services to countless emperors, presidents, kings, queens, and tyrants. He was immortal.

He returned to Alta California in 1846. To become a Californio and to plot and implement the overthrow of Governor Pio Pico. Pico was of Spanish, African, and Indigenous ancestry. He was of mix ancestry. El Cadejo Blanco could not stand Pio Pico since he reminded him of himself. Extravagant, insatiable lust for wealth, loved of gambling, and love of litigation. El Cadejo Blanco also did not like the fact that Governor Pio Pico had Acromegaly growth disease. His head, hands, feet, and other body parts continued to grow non-stop. Similar to Andre the Giant's gigantism. El Cadejo Blanco did not like anyone that could be larger than him. El Cadejo Blanco's ego was larger than the Great Wall of China. He had ingrained evil genetics of envy, selfishness, and jealousy. El Cadejo Blanco advised U.S. troops to invade Mexico and to eventually take over Alta California.

Compounding conflicts led to the Mexican-American War from 1846 to 1848. Eventually both sides decided to sign a peace treaty through the signing of the Treaty of Guadalupe Hidalgo, officially known as the Treaty of Peace, Friendship, Limits and Settlement between the United States of America and the Mexican Republic.

The United States agreed to pay $15 million to Mexico and the U.S. was able to gain/annexed Texas, California, Arizona, Nevada, Utah, and Colorado. To this day, the Treaty of Guadalupe Hidalgo remains an open wound for Mexico. And to this day, it remains a secret that El Cadejo Blanco had possessed President Santana to betray his own people. He gave him a sopa de pito, and el dundo President Santana sold a huge part of Mexico's lands to the United States.

El Cadejo Blanco took advantage of the divisions and hatred between the United States and Mexico. El Cadejo Blanco became an expert in implementing treacherous and wicked political plans.

He discovered that certain viruses could wipe away the Native Americans of North America. He began to purposely spread killer viruses by taking small mice and rats to Native America controlled territories. This was his evil way of causing great sicknesses that would eventually lead to massive deaths. The mice/rats urine and droppings can infect humans causing problems with breathing, fatigue, body pains, and intense fevers. Also, the victims develop non-stop coughing attacks.

Only one other individual knew the capacity and depths of evilness of El Cadejo Blanco. And that was El Cadejo

Negro. El Cadejo Negro had discovered that the indigenous native plants could cure some diseases and unintentionally discovered that the Chipilin plant could counter COVID-19.

El Cadejo Negro survived the hambrunas/famines of El Salvador by eating Chipilin. These native plants had magical powers and made El Cadejo Negro, strong beyond believe, and offered protection from the evil spells from his evil twin, El Cadejo Blanco.

Once he implemented the wiping out of the indigenous in the Americas, El Cadejo Blanco teleported him in 1885 to the Congo in Africa. He possessed and took on the appearance of Leopold II, King of the Belgians and Congo, where he ruled until 1908. King Leopold II hated blacks and he enslaved children and adults. He implemented forced labor and if the residents of the Congo would resist or complain, he had ordered the jefes to chop off the hands of the "negros rebeldes e insolentes." Yes, King Leopold II would refer to the black people of the Congo as "those black rebels."

El Cadejo Blanco, disguised as King Leopold II, attended the Berlin Conference in 1884, where the European colonial nations, gave full authority and ownership of the Congo Free State to Leopold II. What an ironic *pinche* name. The Congo was not free. El Cadejo Blanco proposed that he would help the inhabitants of the Congo – which was a true lie. He simply wanted to steal ivory and rubber – to plunder the natural resources by using free/forced labor of the Congo people. It was true disguised slavery, crimes against humanity, a genocide. Between 10 to 15 million Congolese died through this 'force labor.' El Cadejo Blanco made sure to also infect the population with smallpox and sleeping sickness. The Congolese would go sleep with a mild illness, or developing serious sickness, and simply would die in their sleep. Many were worked to death; others would die due to loss of bloods since the Belgium colonizers would punish them by cutting off their hands for not meeting rubber or ivory quotas.

For this point on, El Cadejo Negro will be identified with bold black print. El Cadejo Blanco's name/font will not be bold.

El Cadejo Negro's dream was to find a plant and a cure for racism. That would become his lifelong dream.

El Cadejo Blanco represented disease, war, pain, hatred, envy, jealousy. El Cadejo Blanco represented the essence of racism.

He was involved in the United States' original sin: slavery. That fucker helped to begin the slave trade in 1619. He helped to establish the plantations and even created a manual in regards to how to psychologically and physically torture slaves. He also helped to destroy Native American lives by purposely infecting the indigenous with viruses. He came up with the idea of developing reservations for Native Americans. Once the fertile lands were stolen from the Native Americans they were forced to migrate and live in reservations located in deserts and deserted, isolated lands. Where the Native Americans would not be seen nor heard by the European colonizers/immigrants.

El Cadejo Blanco goal was to create a virus so deadly that it would wipeout most of humanity.

El Cadejo Negro dream was to create world peace and

to find cures to fight deadly viruses being spread by his evil nemesis: El Cadejo Blanco.

El Cadejo Blanco truly believed that the devil had made him special. With an IQ and natural intelligence far beyond any other human. He would refer to ethnic minorities and progressive Whites as "estos perros ignorantes, no saben ni mierda. Yo soy el que tiene valentia y conocimiento de todo." That fucker truly thought that he was superior to anyone. He felt that his European genetics made him extremely intelligent and good looking. He would see himself in the mirror and he would sing Rigo Tovar's song "Perdóname mi amor por ser tan guapo."

He would even put on sunglasses and would let his hair grow just like Rigo Tovar. A Mexican legendary singer who connected with the regular folk. He would meet people and begin singing "Oh que gusto de volverte a ver…"

El Cadejo Blanco knew that we live in a trick society. A society based on tricks and scams. Dog eat dog world. El Cadejo Blanco represented the evil side of humanity. The fuckers who can give you a job, but will not, simply because they enjoy seeing the unemployed suffer. The fuckers that live off tax payer money and programs. The fuckers who think that they are superior than others. The racist. The racist that not only come in white, they come black, yellow, brown, any color you can imagine. As long as they get the opportunity they will fuck you up. They will shoot you in the back. Just like how young Andres Guardado was shot five times in the back by a *brown* Sherriff in Gardena, California. Latino man killing a young Latino man.

A black Superintendent of public schools, becomes the oppressor and feels as if he is the slave owner. Mistreating Black, brown, anyone. A white woman who runs a multi-billion dollar corporation but mistreats and does not promote women into positions of power and a salary disparity continues. An Asian human resources representative who feels that they should not hire other minorities.

America's history is coming back to haunt it. The colonization, slavery, indigenous genocide, anti-immigrant sentiments, coming to the present. Tearing a country apart.

George Floyd, an ordinary man, who is now as relevant and famous as Marting Luther King, Jr. and Malcolm X. Floyd, a gentle giant, who for over eight minutes was tortured to death. His famous last words were "I can't breathe." He pleaded and repeated "I can't breathe" 20 times in a span of eight minutes and 46 seconds. He cried out for his mother while being tortured to death. He would scream out "mama."

El Cadejo Blanco, laughs and adores the pain. He adores the killers, the rapists, the tortures, the domestic abusers. He is one of them.

El Cadejo Negro earns minimum wage, fights for Civil Rights, believes that everyone is equal, helps others, defends the human rights of ordinary people. Does not own magnificent properties. Does not receive acclaim awards from non-profits or government agencies. His dark skin is detested. He is detested. He is perceived as low income. Someone who lives in the urban environment. He is accused of being an imposter. He is well read, speaks clearly and with conviction, and has an extremely high IQ – but he is hated.

His skin color determines his status in society. El Cadejo Negro chooses not to wear Dolce & Gabbana and BRIONI suits. He wears simple clothes.

El Cadejo Blanco, on the other hand, he only wears BRIONI suits and only puts on CREED AVENTUS cologne. He feels that everyone else's shit and piss smells – except his. He only eats saffron, caviar, oysters, white Truffle, Iberico ham, Wagyu beef, Kopi Luwak coffee and Foie gras. He only eats exquisite foods so that his farts will only smell of roses. His favorite dessert is eating lives bats. He wants to absorb the most bacteria and viruses from these bats. To eventually implement his grand master plan. The spreading of the Coronavirus, COVID-19.

He adores money and power above all else. The dollar is his God. He makes up stories and creates rumors to destroy other people's reputation. He loves and emulates Joseph McCarthy. That fucker who destroyed so many people's lives by falsely accusing them of being Communist. He was simply a drunkard who had hatred and evil in his heart.

Moving onto the present.

El Cadejo Blanco came up with a master plan to create havoc throughout the world. He would help to create a monstrous virus – and he would patent and trademark the cure. Since he would help to create it – then, he would know the ingredients necessary to be included in the vaccine. El Cadejo Blanco's hunger for money was to make trillions of dollars in profits – when he would sale his vaccine to billions of human beings. He howled with laughter and joy in regards to all of the pain and suffering that he would create, worldwide.

El Cadejo Blanco was an evil genius. First, he bought extensive lands/properties in El Salvador, throughout Central America, Chiapas, and Southern Mexico. To secure the contracts with the farmers who would plant and grow las plantas de Chipilin. The chief ingredient in the vaccine to fight the deadly virus.

The gang members, criminals running non-profits, corrupt individuals loved El Cadejo Blanco. They would speak to each other through Facebook, Instagram, and WhatsApp and say "El Cadejo Blanco is such a finesse leader, he is so debonair, and well spoken. He says no bad words, he does not talk about sexually explicit topics, and he uses proper grammar."

One wannabe gangster even posted a public message stating "we kidnap, rape, torture, and kill innocent men, women, and children. But we do not cross the line of using graphic language or bad words in our emails, social media postings, or greenlighted hit jobs. We are honorable men."

Yes, honorable men, recruiting children to teach them to torture and extort their own people.

El Cadejo Blanco knew that people could be easily manipulated and brainwashed and he even would quote Saddam Hussein by saying "Starve your dog and it will always follow you."

His next grand plan was to become the wealthiest drug trafficker and pimp in the United States. But in order to become the biggest pimp in the U.S. and the world, he needed to take control of the secrets ingredients that were included in the vaccine to eradicate COVID-19. What he did not realize was that his motherfucker goody two shoes brother, El Cadejo Negro had already patented and trademarked el Chipilin. One of the most powerful plants in the world that could counter the negative effects of various viruses.

He came up with an ingenious plan, he would apply to become the first ever Latino to run The Cherry Club. The most powerful environmental group in the United States. He would place Latinx in his employment application so that the Human Resources Department would not know whether he was a man or a woman. And to be up to date with the trendiest politically correct term. To be hip.

He would type his resume on natural recycled paper and would use green font to showcase his commitment to the Green Movement. He told himself, while admiring his beauty, "should I go to the meeting in white or black, or light brown? That fucker was a true genio. He could use his chameleon powers to change skin and hair color when convenient.

This is something that El Cadejo Negro refused to partake in. He wanted to remain true to his African heritage and to keep his skin/hair black. To be consistent and authentic. He wanted to achieve all of his dreams by maintaining his true identity and God given skin/hair color.

El Cadejo Blanco had no scruples nor morals. The fucker hacked the email accounts of the board members and hiring committee members. That way he could see what they were saying about him and to also see if they had any secret political deals or affairs that he could use in the future to manipulate them. He also realized that they were planning to have a racially balanced hiring and interview committees.

Ten members would make the ultimate decision. 7 Whites, 1 Black, 1 Asian, and 1 Latino. That way they could say that they had three minorities. Of course, they were light skin minorities and fulfilled the 1% quota.

El Cadejo Blanco decided to take on a light brown skin tone. That way he could please both, the Whites and the three minorities. He created an app that could detect his accent decibel level. He wanted it to be exactly at 50% hint of Spanish language accent. That way the committee members could check off that he was fluent in English.

He wore his most exquisite suit for the interview. Of course, made of recycled cotton.

The interview was held in the mansion known as Antilia, the world's most expensive mansion in the world. Located in Mumbai. The developers that built Antilia are great supporters of the World Wildlife Fund for Nature.

The seven Whites were top administrators paid well over $500,000 per year, the Latina employee was the receptionist and she was paid a whopping $30,000. The Black employee was the of the Equality and Fairness Environmental Office, and the Asian was the accountant who had a PhD from Harvard University, a Master's degree from Stanford University, and a BA from Oxford University. All of his degrees were in American Literature but he was naturally gifted with numbers since his parents from Arcadia had enrolled him in the Kumon Math and Reading Center of San Gabriel. The Latina receptionist had received her BA from Occidental College and had obtained a Master's Degree from

UC Berkeley. The Black individual on the hiring committee had obtain his BA from Howard University and Master's and PhD degrees from Columbia University. The seven White committee members were individually wealthy and were your typical Trust Fund Babies. They all had paid William "Rick" Singer, founder of the Edge College & Career Network to get them into USC and other top tier universities.

El Cadejo Blanco chose to wear a light green, Cannabis made tailor suit. His tie was made of recycled bicycle tires and his shoes were hand made by exploited children from India. He looked magnifico.

When he walked into the interview conference room, he wore a torero hat. The hiring committee was in awe to see such a debonair gentleman. His accent was exquisite and pleasing to the ears of the interviewers. They actually became nervous in the presence of El Cadejo Blanco. He word torero tight pants to the interview to showcase his big balls. Sus huevos de perro caliente.

The committee asked the young Latina token to ask the first question, she cleared her throat and said "Excuse me Mr. Cadejo, you come from a tiny, almost invisible, insignificant little developing country, El Salvador." El Cadejo growled. He quickly took the offensive and to told Ms. Tokenita, "excuse me, it is pronounced El Salvador, we produce the most exquisite coffee in the world and George Melendez Wright, mi primo, was a Sierra Club member and he was leader in helping solidify the National Park Service. He just happened to have attended Berkeley and probably subsidized your education there." He winked at Ms. Tokenita and concluded by saying "Game, Set, Match." The seven white interviewees where truly impressed, a Latino making a referral to tennis. They each texted each other with a thumbs up. Practically he was hired. El Cadejo Blanco's hacking ability had discovered that the seven White members were fans of Wimbledon and that was the key to gain their support. He had to come across as a tennis connoisseur.

The president of the board of directors told El Cadejo Blanco "you did exceptionally well. We will call you tomorrow to let you if you will be leading the Cherry Club."

El Cadejo Blanco's master plan was coming together. Once he would become the leader of the Cherry Club he would seek his ultimate goal, to be invited to become a board member of Pfizer. The most powerful and wealthiest drug making corporation in the world. That way he could use Pfizer as the producer and distributor of the El Chipilin vaccine to counter the Hantavirus, Coronavirus, Ebola, Marburg virus, Rabies, HIV, Smallpox, Influenza, Dengue, Rotavirus, SARS-CoV, SARS-COV2 (Coronavirus), and MERS-CoV.

El Cadejo Blanco knew that once he would obtain the patent and trademark of the EL CHIPILIN vaccine, he would automatically become a trillionaire.

Leader of the Cherry Club, a powerful board member of Pfizer, and a motherfuckin trillionaire! His goal was sweet revenge against La Siguanaba. Who now was serving as Pope to the Catholic Church.

First, he would help to spread the Hantavirus, Coronavirus, Ebola, Dengue, and MERS-CoV. He wanted the human population to suffer and die. His demonic side took great joy to see people get fevers, bleed to death, develop deadly inflammations, and he ultimately enjoyed seeing people die of respiratory illnesses. He loved to see people cry out and say, "I cannot breathe, no puedo respirar." He would howl with joy and laughter. His eyes would turn bright red – you could see the pits of hell through his eyes. His testicles would quiver and grow enormously since seeing people die would provoke erections. He would get sexually aroused to the point that he would ejaculate without even engaging in sexual intercourse. He was like Derek Chauvin, the Minneapolis police officer that murdered George Floyd by placing his knee on Floyd's neck and pretty much murdered him while he pleaded "I can't breathe." Derek Chauvin's little dirty secret is that he is a sadomasochist. He loved to rub his penis while he would choke his female or male lovers. He was an undercover sadomasochist who ejaculated while he tortured his lovers or people that he would arrest.

El Cadejo Blanco avoided remembering "The Little Ones," El Cipitio and El Duende. He detested both of them since they had attempted to permanently murder him by boiling his ass in a *sopa de pata.* He would play *Tarde o Temprano* de Camilo Sesto to forget their little asses. When he would get really fucked up with Crystal Meth, he would blast *Tomame o Dejame* de Mocedades y *Que Mala* by Los Bukis. A song he would secretly dedicate to La Siguanaba. That evil fucker still had a crush on the big titty mama.

El Cadejo Negro had to make sure that no one would find out his deepest dark secret. He was a paid FBI/CIA informant. Not just any low-level informant but a highly paid professionally trained spy. His gift - his ability to shift skin color. He had developed a goody two-shoes image of being a fighter for Civil Rights and Human Rights, which gave him unprecedented access to such stalwart organizations such as the National Association for the Advancement of Colored People (NAACP), American Civil Liberties Union (ACLU), UNIDOS (formerly known as the National Council of La Raza), and Asian Americans Advancing Justice. He had infiltrated all of these organizations and many more. He had even infiltrated Russia's president Putin by pretending to be a black fur loyal dog that Putin would use to intimidate foreign presidential visitors such as Germany's Chancellor Angela Merkel.

El Cadejo Blanco was simply a colonizador y explotador. He also had the ability to shift colors but mostly remained white since he detested to look darker. He was a White Supremacist and he would spread that philosophy by spreading viruses and becoming the leader of the Cherry Club. A great outfit to promote stabilizing overpopulation. He would also use the Cherry Club to endorse and support Pfizer's evil plans to patent and take ownership of all the Chipilin plants that currently exist in the world.

The motherfuckin war was on. El Cadejo Negro versus El Cadejo Blanco. Since they were twins, the devil's genetics existed within both.

El Cadejo Negro had to beat his twin brother, El Cadejo Blanco. His heroic side wanted revenge and reparations regarding the slave trade imposed by El Cadejo Blanco.

El Cadejo Negro was given a mission and ordered to apply to become superintendent of the Los Angeles Unified School District (LAUSD). That way, he could become a great salesperson and representative for the billion-dollar publishing industry. As superintendent, he would have unfettered access to select and include only certain books, considered safe, and he would get his favorite buddy authors to get book contracts with the billion-dollar publishers and with the school district. Then, those same books would be adopted by the California State Board of Education, which would make school districts predisposed to adopt and require those same books, statewide. Ethnic studies books were purposely excluded, especially Central American books. El Cadejo Negro would get a cut from the book profits and he would have extra money to pay more informants for his spy missions – specifically to counter the efforts of El Cadejo Blanco.

El Cadejo Negro was a perfect spy for the FBI/CIA to infiltrate and destroy The Black Panthers. El Cadejo Negro even won a "Hero Award" from the FBI for plotting the murder of Fred Hampton, who was classified as the Black Messiah by the FBI/CIA. Edgar Hoover knew that he had hired his best man, El Cadejo Negro. He acted humble and meek when he met Fred Hampton. El Cadejo Negro used slang to flatter Mr. Hampton by telling him, "my man, you are a special cat. I want to be your bodyguard and I will give my life for you. You are a beautiful and intelligent man who can become bigger than Martin Luther King, Jr. and Gandhi." Mr. Hampton was blown away with the flattery and told El Cadejo Negro, "you are now hired; you are my main bodyguard." That was the biggest mistake that Fred Hampton made in his short life. He did not realize that he had hired the other son of The Prince of Darkness who would betray him.

One night, Fred Hampton and his Black Panther friends went to sleep. His bodyguard, El Cadejo Negro, had already drugged Fred Allen Hampton with powerful sleeping pills. To completely knock him out into a deep sleep. When the police arrived, a death sentence had already been approved by the FBI and Edgar J. Hoover. He was shot to death dozens of times. He was murdered in cold blood. El Cadejo Negro implemented the COINTELPRO plan. To spy on, follow, create disinformation, and to ultimately murder all of the Black Panther Leaders.

El Cadejo Negro had no remorse since his evil genes were more powerful than his skin color.

One night, El Cadejo Negro and El Cadejo Blanco, had a philosophical conversation at midnight. They came to an agreement that skin and fur color should not matter. That God and the Devil made humans and animals with a diversity of colors. El Cadejo Negro even quoted Martin Luther King, Jr. by reciting "I have a dream. That my four little children will one day live in a nation where they will not be judged by the color of their skin but by the content of their character." El Cadejo Blanco was impressed. He said, "think about it, evil comes in all colors. John F. Kennedy and John Lennon were both murdered by white men." They both howled with laughter as they drank some Guaro y Rum con Coca-Cola.

El Cadejo Blanco concluded their conversation by saying, "we have a long fucking way to go in relation to Race in America. COVID 19 and other viruses/diseases will continue to expose human's stupidity in relation to hating other people based on their skin color and Race/ethnic/national origin identification."

The truth of the matter is that all humans are mixed. Most scientists agree that humanity initiated in Africa. No matter what, all humans, including the White Supremacists, have African roots. The fuckers may never want to admit it, but it is a reality. Humans have migrated for eternity.

It's just that the United States was founded on principles of hating and exploiting the indigenous and slaves. America's original sin continues to haunt her to this day. Also, El Cadejo Negro y El Cadejo Blanco also agreed that even within certain ethnic groups, hatred exists due to the ignorance of dislike towards national origin. For example, do Mexicans and Salvadorans get along? Do Palestinians and Israelites get along? Do Iranians and Saudi Arabians get along? Do Japanese and Koreans get along? Do Armenians and Azerbaijans get along? Do Chinese and Japanese get along? The list can go and on. Human ignorance goes beyond skin color. Do Blacks kill Blacks? Do Latinos kill Latinos? Do Blacks kill Latinos? Do Latinos kill Blacks? Do Latino cops kill Latino community members? Do Black cops kill Black community members? Do Whites kill Whites? Hell yes!!!

El Cadejo Blanco was the creator of the *Divide and Conquer* strategic plans. El Cadejo Blanco's strategy to sow death and divisions through COVID-19 has worked perfectly. He even possessed and took the persona of Derek Chauvin. He knew that a video recording of George Floyd's murder would create fury, to the point of leading to protests and riots.

El Cadejo Blanco was ecstatic that his plan to spread COVID-19 and Race wars would help him to gain more power with the Cherry Club, Pfizer, and that he would evolve to become the White Messiah for America. He wanted to be nicknamed our *modern-day John Muir.* He loved John Muir to the point that he would carry Muir's photo in his wallet. He loved John Muir's racist beliefs and that he was able to steal lands from the indigenous. He felt that Muir was a genius since he painted himself as a natural resources and nature savior to cover up his hatred towards minorities and visionary plan of buying land to fund White Supremacy efforts cloaked in conservation and environmental protection efforts. Whites felt that they were naturally superior and that they could simply steal lands and resources from minorities – and then hire high priced attorneys to develop exploitative contracts in the music industry, book publishing industry, property development and real estate transactions, food/agricultural industry, and all other careers where Whites are the naturally gifted bosses. They simply hire docile, and yes, minority men and women who are willing to do the bidding and exploitation for the White man.

El Cadejo Negro and El Cadejo Blanco symbolized the stratification and patriarchal exploitative system established by the founders of America. Los perros de America Founders owned slaves; and many raped the female slaves and impregnated them with *mixed* children. Thomas Jefferson is a perfect example. He had a secret relationship with Sally Hemings, one of his slaves. Jefferson and Hemings had multiple children together. This has been one of the best kept secrets in American history. But it is a fact and it is now public knowledge. America's secret, taboo history.

Now getting back to El Cadejo Blanco's evil plan. He flew to Wuhan, China. He wanted to see firsthand if humans were torturing and eating dogs and other exotic animals such as Pangolins and Bats. Once he arrived, El Cadejo Blanco went into a rage. He began to bark, howl, and cry. He could not believe his eyes. All sorts of animals were caged and were being sold to the highest bidder. He saw how people were eating live bats. Humans were paying thousands of dollars and renminbi to purchase Pangolins. Simply to cook them and to eat them for aphrodisiac purposes.

El Cadejo Blanco decided to go back to his John Muir grassroots organizing motto "Power to the Animals." El Cadejo Blanco convened a secret meeting, specifically with the bats and Pangolins. He offered them an opportunity that they could not refuse: to help him spread a virus/disease that would take revenge upon the greedy and corrupt humans. First, El Cadejo Blanco took testimony from the bats and Pangolins to document their mistreatment and torture. He was outraged to hear how bats were being eaten alive and boiled in soups. Then, he got more pissed off to hear how Pangolins were being trafficked throughout the world. He asked the bats and Pangolins if they were willing to begin spreading a virus. They agreed. Second, he asked the Pangolin leader who had escaped the cage at the Wuhan wet market, to decide the name of the virus. The Pangolin started talking gangster since he had seen American Me multiple times through Chinese pirated DVD videos. The Pangolin said, "ese, we are gonna call this shit el CORONA virus. Para la raza. For the Anglos, we gonna call this little fucker, COVID-19."

The Pangolin said that he was tired of being kept in cages and having to roll into a little ball to take protection and to hide from humans. He started to cry and added, "those fuckers wanna shank me ese and I ain't done nada to them. Pinches cobardes."

El Cadejo Blanco, El Bat leader, and the Pangolin leader, all signed a blood oath. To begin a destructive rampage against humans. Los perros, los murcielagos, y los Pangolins weren't going to take shit from no one, no more!!

They even decided to start their own diverse gang called CBP 13 and their motto was "somos pocos per locotes."

They agreed with Pope Francis. It was revenge by nature. Nature, which includes animals, have been so denigrated, tortured, and murdered in a merciless manner. Human greed at Wuhan market was a perfect example of how animals are trafficked to be sold to be eaten by greedy humans. Motherfuckin poachers! They hunt animals such as elephants to cut off and steal their ivory, especially in countries such as Cameroon and Republic of the Congo. Poachers are armed criminals who catch gorillas for their meat (the poachers and buyers believe that the meat from gorillas will give them more strength) and body parts – sold to be made into trophies. The Pangolin scales are highly sought after by men who have erectile dysfunction. Let us not forget Spain's Juan Carlos who loved to hunt and kill elephants while the Spanish population was economically hurting and jobless.

These poachers destroy forests, species, and anything that gets in their way. We depend on the forests and plants that provide oxygen for humans.

El Cadejo Blanco is an evil fucker but he cried and cried when he saw how elephants, gorillas, bats, and Pangolins were cut into pieces. Blood dripping everywhere. He saw how people in China and other countries thought it was cute to eat live bats. Cutting their wings, bite after bite. The humans laughed as they ate the poor bats, alive.

That traumatic experience made El Cadejo Blanco swear that he would take revenge against the greedy humans. Those fucking humans whose God is money! They love money above anything else. Their houses of worship are the banks. They love bankers, developers, stock market, and anything that smells of money. They will sell their own soul for a dollar.

El Cadejo Blanco told the Bat leaders and Pangolin leaders to begin infecting humans with COVID-19. To travel far and wide.

He agreed with them to begin the infection during the Chinese New Year celebrations in China. He knew that tens of millions would travel to China to celebrate and then they would leave China and they would return to the United

States, Italy, Spain, Australia, everywhere where the Chinese diaspora had settled in.

El Cadejo Negro wanted to teach a lesson to the G7 country leaders: Canada, France, Germany, Italy, Japan, United Kingdom, and the United States. He was tired of seeing these countries reaping the benefits of their colonization enrichment efforts and continual extraction of natural resources and food from developing countries.

He wanted the spoiled humans to stop adoring and idolizing the actors, actresses, and sports figures who were millionaires and billionaires. Who were contributing in buying mansions with over 50 to 100 rooms while only one or two people lived there. Why would any human need a gigantic mansion to live in? Why would a human need more than a million dollars a year to live on? While the working poor barely make $10,000 or $15,000 a year. That is how the working class in the ghettos of America have been getting by. The poor whites of the South – who make minimum wage and also earn less than $15,000 to subsist on. They cannot afford medical care. The rich keep getting all of the money, including the taxpayer funds from the Payroll Protection Program (PPP). Over 3 million wealthy individuals got over $5 million each from the PPP Federal Funds. While the working poor was not even eligible.

El Cadejo Blanco had several revelations. First, he realized that he has a conscience.

Then, he looked in the mirror and realized that El Cadejo Blanco and El Cadejo Negro were one and the same. That he was a twin!!!

Except that at night, they would shift colors. They would become possessed. The Prince of Darkness and God was within them. They both had to fight to control their evil side.

Once the Prince of Darkness would decide to possess either one, they would become tremendously evil. Regardless of their skin color, El Cadejo Negro was tired of the social constructs that black is perceived as evil and that white is right.

El Cadejo Blanco also had to face his white privilege and contributions in the destruction of humanity through slavery and colonization. White supremacy was a true fact. What was difficult for El Cadejo Blanco, was to admit his prejudices and natural racist tendencies.

He was ashamed of all the public-school districts, private schools, charter schools, public and private colleges and universities that had produced experts in the exploitation of humanity. Experts in running corporations, businesses, non-profits, and labor unions, that eventually became corrupted through evil and greedy individuals. World leaders would become infected with COVID-19.

El CBP 13 was going to teach these individuals a lesson through COVID-19. The import and export industry would be decimated. Humans would be forced to take refuge in their homes and elected officials would have to impose lockdown/stay at home orders. Social distancing at 6 to 27 feet would become mandatory.

Banks would lose profits; McDonalds and Coca-Cola would be negatively impacted since hundreds of millions of people would become unemployed and not able to afford a

Big Mac and a Coke. The car industry would begin to lose profits.

COVID-19 would begin to mutate. It would begin to appear to be a monster with multiple heads. El Cadejo Blanco, El Bat, and The Pangolin, joined forces in spreading multiple viruses. They even hired hit mice and rats to spread the Hantavirus. Their job was to jump into suitcases that would travel to other countries. Fuck, some of the mice were so bold that they would skip Homeland Security and would sneak and crawl into airplanes. To spread fleas among the passengers. To further spread the Hantavirus. The mice/rats were given a special assignment: to shit on the humans who would not wear masks. The ones that felt that their civil liberties were being stepped on since they were true Americans, they did not need to wear no fucking masks. The gangster mice would purposely take a shit on the mask of the rebels who refused to wear one. The little, tiny caca/fecal matter had the Hantavirus.

Soon, the viruses were spreading worldwide. "Excellent," said El Cadejo Blanco. "Nobody is gonna fuck with the CBP 13. Fuck them humans," El Cadejo Blanco howled.

His plan was working perfectly. He just had to get the approval of the Patent, Trademark, and sole ownership of the vaccine to cure these viruses/diseases. El pinche Chipilin.

El Cadejo Blanco loved Bill Clinton. A white Anglo Saxon Cadejo. He loved him so much to the point of quoting him by stating "I'll be there for you until the last dog dies." He would laugh and laugh and conclude "I'm the fucking last dog to die." What people did not know was that El

Cadejo Blanco was Bill Clinton's closest friend and advisor while he served as president. He was so tight with Clinton, that he actually advised him on how to survive the Monica Lewinsky scandal. Bill Clinton, Chelsey Clinton, and Hillary Clinton even invited and took El Cadejo Blanco to Martha's Vineyard on family vacations. There, El Cadejo Blanco would take long beach walks with Bill Clinton. To give him advice and fortitude. El Cadejo Blanco told him to just tell the American people "I am a sinner." That strategy ultimately worked. He admitted his little adventure with Lewinsky, and he did solidify his nickname, *The Comeback Kid.* Senator Trent Lott (prominent Conservative Republican) never quite knew how Clinton survived the impeachment process. What Republicans and Democrats never knew was Clinton's personal secret weapon, El Cadejo Blanco. He was always at Clinton's side during a crisis. He was impeached by the House of Representatives but not to be removed from office. The American people did not give a fuck that Clinton had received a blow job in the White House. Most Americans actually felt that was pretty cool.

The evil side of El Cadejo Blanco, particularly wanted to reduce the population of the Latinos and Blacks in the United States. By infecting them in an extremely wider margin, since they are America's frontline workers. He was pleasing the White supremacists. They were true followers of John Muir who also detested minorities, especially the indigenous who owned the lands. Muir had also retained the consulting services of El Cadejo Blanco. Of course, dumb asses just saw El Cadejo Blanco as a lowly dog.

They do not realize that El Cadejo Blanco has been the top advisor and close friend to world leaders such as Russia's Putin, former U.S. president Bill Clinton, and even a top advisor to former president Barack Obama. Of course, he went undercover as Bo, a Portuguese Water Dog. He chose to be colochito and was even biracial. And that is why he got along so tight with Obama. They even had a secret fist/paw bump. Not even the CIA, FBI, National Security Agency (NSA), and Obama's bodyguards knew that El Cadejo Blanco/Negro was disguised as *Bo*.

For W. Bush, he went undercover as *Barney*, a Scottish Terrier. His father, George H.W. Bush had El Cadejo as an advisor and even played a low-key role by serving as *Sully*, a yellow Labrador service dog for H.W. Bush. His job was to protect, advise, and comfort H.W. Bush in retirement.

Dr. Stella Immanuel was one of the doctors that knew that the indigenous vaccine against COVID-19 is a potluck of garlic, red onion, cola de caballo, limes, oranges, and ginger and El Cadejo Blanco had stolen some of her secrets by hacking her INTEL Microsoft Word laptop computer.

El Cadejo Blanco did not want the average folks to know of these home remedies and potential vaccine against COVID-19. That is why he started a rumor that Dr. Stella Immanuel wanted to promote mysterious demon and alien brews that came from mysterious African villages. He painted her as a crazy voodoo doctor.

El Cadejo Blanco started referring to Dr. Immanuel, that "crazy bitch witch doctor." The National Organization of Women (NOW) went into a tailspin once they read El

Cadejo Blanco's quote in *The Enquirer*. They were outraged that a male dog would refer to a woman in such a derogatory manner. The board members of NOW began to call and email the board of the Cherry Club to get rid of that *machista dog*. The leadership of NOW felt that this was the perfect campaign to review their membership base and to gain more supporters from the Latino and black communities. Their strategy was to take away members from the Cherry Club, especially Latina and black women.

NOW created an Instagram, Facebook, Snap Chat, and Twitter campaign titled "Boycott the Machista Dog – El Cadejo Blanco."

What people did not realize was that La Siguanaba was on the board of directors of NOW. She was also a major donor. She told the leaders of NOW during a tea meeting "let's get that bitch El Cadejo Blanco. We have to cut his balls off – neuter him with no anesthesia."

The NOW leadership recruited Oprah Winfrey to join their campaign in denouncing El Cadejo Blanco – The Machista Dog. Oprah became the best and most effective spokesperson in denouncing El Cadejo Blanco.

El Cadejo Blanco had to fight back with his paws and claws. He hired a top consulting media firm to help him appear to be pro-feminist.. He hired Dick Morris to conduct polling and Morris advised him to call Joe Biden to offer his support. Biden started to laugh and immediately stated "how is my Machista Dog?" El Cadejo Blanco rebutalled by stating "how is my Mr. Women Hugger?" Biden quickly decided to code switch to Mr. Righteous. He told El Cadejo that he had to support his female vice-presidential candidate. And El Cadejo Blanco said "done."

Dick Morris also recommended to El Cadejo Blanco to join the Black Lives Matter movement and to code switch to black fur/skin. El Cadejo Blanco hugged and gave Morris a sloppy, wet kiss and said, "you are a fucking genius." They also discussed that El Cadejo Blanco should go on the Ellen show. To tell the American public his humble beginnings, his positive contributions in protecting our environment through the Cherry Club, to highlight that he is the first dark skinned leader of the Cherry Club, and that he was a humanitarian by serving on the board of Pfizer. Pfizer gave El Cadejo Blanco an unrestricted funding pot of money $2 billion. He could throw money at any individual or group that he would need to *influence.*

Ellen DeGeneres was ecstatic to have El Cadejo Blanco on her show. She was intrigued in relation to all of the rumors that existed in regard to El Cadejo Blanco's mythology and corruption. She could connect with him at a deep level. They both could be mean-spirited and vindictive if anyone crossed them. Ellen figured that she needed an ally like El Cadejo Blanco to be in her corner when it would possibly get hot in the kitchen.

El Cadejo Blanco was driven in a limousine to the Ellen show. He wanted to be perceived as royalty. He even purchased a crown that he could wear to showcase a symbolism of power and royalty lineage. It was also a subliminal message regarding the Coronavirus – which translates to the Crown virus. For the interview on Ellen, El

Cadejo Blanco decided to code switch to the image of Bo, Obama's dog. He could be white and black – and appeal to both White America and Black America. He figured that including Asians and Latinos would just complicate a national discussion related to race, gender issues, and health disparities. He wanted to keep it simple. Who do you think came up with the slogan "it's the economy, stupid," it was none other than El Cadejo Blanco. He came up with that idea while he walked on the beach with Bill Clinton.

Ellen could not wait. Her producers had developed whopper questions. The audience could not wait to finally see El Cadejo Blanco in his true nature: as a Machista Dog. The White and Black women in the audience were expecting to see a thug full of tattoos and scars. Ellen ordered her producers to find two Latinas to include in the audience. Ellen told her producers, "they better speak English. If not, I will fire your asses!"

However, once Ellen called El Cadejo Blanco to come on stage, they were speechless. He came out as a Portuguese Water Dog. To highlight his European background and colonizer/slave trader background. Of course, the audience could care less about El Cadejo Blanco's history of being a slave trader and human trafficker. They were in awe. One white lady spoke to the black lady next to her at the Ellen show and said, "how could El Cadejo be a racist if he is mixed, black and white?" The black lady said, "girl, don't you know your history? The white man has always used Uncle Tom's to betray their own community."

El Cadejo came out with his head held high. The crown

that he was wearing was magnificent. It was the original crown that was placed upon King Afonso V of Portugal. No wonder, he truly did look like King Afonso V. The most powerful and wealthiest King of Europe during the 1400s. The lineage of El Cadejo was connected to Afonso.

Ellen had prepared a magnificent seating arrangement and she even played Queen's *We Are the Champions,* while El Cadejo slowly walked to be seated.

The first question that Ellen threw at El Cadejo Blanco, was "are you the leader of a gang called CBP 13?" El Cadejo Blanco started to blink nonstop. His blue eyes turned bright red and he responded "Ellen, my dear, is it true that you mistreat your staff?" Ellen was humiliated and turned bright dark red, like a beet, since she was so embarrassed that a Machista Dog had called her out on her television show.

Ellen cleared her throat and decided to throw a softball, puffy question. "How do you feel to be the first dark person leading the Cherry Club?" and El Cadejo Blanco responded "I feel magnificent. We have billions of dollars in our budget and I get to fly throughout the United States and the world. I get to eat organic dog food."

The audience burst into laughter. That question saved Ellen. Then, Ellen asked a controversial question "are you anti-women Mr. Cadejo?" and El Cadejo Blanco said "well, let me be clear. I am not anti-women. Half of my staff at the Cherry Club are women. We have an equal opportunity and employment policy and we support Affirmative Action. We also give money to civil rights and human rights causes. As a matter of fact, I have a check here."

Ellen was surprised and asked, "a check for who?" and El Cadejo Blanco said "it is a $1 billion donation from Pfizer to the National Organization for Women (NOW). It is for NOW to fight machismo and to eradicate racism within NOW and other feminists' organizations." Ellen was shocked.

Ellen turned to the audience and one lady stood up to share with the audience. "I am a NOW member, and I want to thank El Cadejo Blanco for his kindness. We can use that $1 billion to develop more ZOOM workshops and training sessions to eradicate racism. We are so excited! Thank you, your majesty Cadejo."

El Cadejo Blanco said, "no problem. I have to make amends for my machista lifestyle. After all, I am a true dog." The audience fell off their chairs with laughter.

Then, to add more significance to the Ellen show, El Cadejo Blanco said that the Cherry Club would donate $100 million to the Ellen show – to conduct fair treatment of employees and guests on her show. Ellen was truly grateful and thanked El Cadejo Blanco and concluded the show "El Cadejo has made history today. He made amends with NOW and also displayed, through royalty by being a wonderful philanthropist. With this $100 million, we will be able to continue hiring employment law attorneys to continue to protect my brand and image. Thank you, Mr. Cadejo Blanco."

El Cadejo Blanco was so generous that he threw in a lifetime of free *Kibbles 'n Bits* to all of the audience members. He said, "all women, men, minority and nonminority, deserve a lifetime of free *Kibbles 'n Bits"* and walked off with his shiny crown. He raised his left hand, with a fist, and shouted "Dog Power."

Now, El Cadejo Blanco could focus on solidifying his power through the Cherry Club and Pfizer. To ingratiate himself with other environmental groups, he would create a pot of money to donate to the other environmental and environmental justice groups. He figured "what the fuck, I can get a tax write-off from the IRS and get favors from these environmental groups if I ever run for political office." He would also use the donations to appease and to keep the environmental justice groups from truly organizing in polluted states such as California, Texas, Georgia, Louisiana, North Carolina, and many others.

He wanted the Cherry Club to be a country club type of non-profit organization. They would dine and wine the donors at elite country clubs and mansions that would waste tons of water every day just to keep the front lawns green and lush. They also had magnificent pools that were filled with imported water from Fiji and France.

He donated $500,000 to Latino and black non-profits. He knew that greedy board members and self-serving executive directors would eventually plunder, waste, and use the $500,000 to pay themselves extravagant salaries and bonuses. In the process, making sure to run the non-profits into the ground, bleeding it dry, and then, conveniently closing the non-profits because the Secretary of State and IRS does not give a shit when non-profits shutter their doors once they have plundered and taken the last cent from the bank.

Some of these sneaky executive directors and accountants were so advanced, they would copy a playbook from the dictators. Right before they would leave power, they would hire part-time paper shredding companies to destroy all of the paperwork and budgets. To cover their tracks and leave no traces of the extraction and pilfering of donated money.

El Cadejo Blanco would howl with laughter since he knew that most humans were seeking monetary gain, wealth, material possessions, and prestige at all costs. They pretended to be in favor of civil rights and human rights, but they sure did fucking live in extravagant homes, away from the most polluted and ghettoized areas. They wanted to make sure that White folks would see them as if they made it out of the ghetto. At the fancy wine parties, they would tell the White billionaires and descendants of slave owners and murderers of the indigenous population "thank you for your generosity in donating to our non-profit. Without your help, we could not survive. You are a kind philanthropist and we will nominate you for the "Crumbs Award." The billionaires would simply smile and would say "My Latino assistant says that I will have to leave early to get on my private jet to begin my vacation at the private island that I just purchased. It is fabulous. Do visit sometime. We have taken extraordinary measures to keep COVID-19 away from my island."

Some board members of the Cherry Club, some white mainstream environmental leaders, and Black, Latino, and Asian environmental justice activists began to resent, envy, and develop great jealousy towards El Cadejo Blanco. They were angry that El Cadejo Blanco could fly and chill with

Jeff Bezos, Bill Gates, Bernard Arnault, Warren Buffet, Larry Ellison, Amancio Ortega, Mark Zuckerberg, Jim Rob, and Alice Walton.

They were like, "who does that coconut think he is? He is just brown on the outside but white on the inside. Look at his buddies, they white. I went to USC and I got my law degree and I am from the hood. That crooked fool comes from the Gates of Hell. He ain't no true minority. I'm the true minority!"

El Cadejo tweeted and stated "Why is everyone claiming to be from South Central Los Angeles now? Before, they claimed to be from West Los Angeles. Now that my ten buddies are giving money away, all of a sudden they are from South Central Los Angeles!"

The power of El Cadejo lied in the ability to *pass*. To *pass* as White or Black, or even both. He could code switch – from ghetto gangster to royal gentleman. Whatever the fuck he chose. He was a twin. One evil, and one kind and generous.

The evil Cadejo had unleashed the 1918/1919 Blue Plague that ravished the world. Between 50 to 100 million human beings died.

Present day, El Cadejo Blanco had unleashed COVID-19. On a worldwide scale.

The developed countries and the developing countries, all were affected. Many had to go into lockdown since the virus spread like wildfire.

The racist white Cadejo, El Cadejo Blanco, specifically contributed to the spreading of the virus in Black and Latino communities. Just like environmental racism. Where were the most polluting companies and waste incinerators placed throughout the United States? Next to Black and Latino communities. Causing great air and water contamination. Many of these polluting corporations caused cancer in millions of human beings.

El Cadejo Blanco was a consultant for the polluters. His "cherry on the top" achievement was becoming a powerful board member of Pfizer. He requested for Pfizer to patent, copyright, and trademark the name of the CHIPILIN plant. Which they did successfully. Homeland Security had obtained special privileges from the U.S. Customs and Border Protection. Only El Cadejo Blanco (via Pfizer) had the authority to export and import chipilin plants. That fucker was a genius. He was doing what Johnson & Johnson and other billion-dollar corporations had done in the past. To take natural plants from the indigenous and commercialize them by making them via a mixture of chemicals – to patent and to sell at extremely high prices. Then, through time, the prices were lowered to be able to market and sell to billions of new buyers.

The following are drugs derived from natural plants: Opium poppy, which is now massively produced as heroin, morphine, and codeine. The famous Coca leaves that are used to produce cocaine. Ephedra sinica is used to produce Sudafed and Meth. Willow bark is used to produce aspirin. Sassafras root is used to make ecstasy.

Add chipilin, that is used with a mixture of garlic, red onion, cola de caballo, limes, oranges, and ginger. To produce the vaccines against COVID-19 and other viruses created and mutated through the CBP 13 gang.

El Cadejo Blanco's side projects included heading up CBP 13 and controlling the politics of the Mexican Mafia, the Black Gorrilla Family, and the Aryan Brotherhood. These prison gangs knew that the new mero mero was El Cadejo Blanco.

They knew he held the keys to power and that he was one of the most elusive criminals in the history of the world. They admired and paid homage to him since they knew he was directly derived from the Prince of Darkness/The Devil.

El Cadejo Blanco created the trade of CHIPILIN – which quickly out spaced the Opium trade. Everyone wanted a piece of the action. The governments of various countries requested private meetings with El Cadejo. Also, criminal syndicates such as the Russian Mafia, Chinese Mafia, Italian Mafia, and other syndicates, also requested private meetings with El Cadejo.

El Cadejo was busy. But when Richard Branson called from Virgin Airlines, he answered his cell phone right away and began by saying "Richard, baby, what took you so long to call me? You're my favorite man. You protect the rights of animals and advocate for humans to not kill animals and you also advocate for humans to stop eating meat. Now we are talking my man."

Branson began with his exquisite British accent by saying "We have to address Climate Change and thank you for your kind words. Yes, I believe in the efforts to protect animals like you. We need clean energy and a green economy. And

I truly believe the Chipilin plant is the answer to protect us from viruses. It is a win-win. We plant Chipilin throughout the world and I offer you my Virgin airplanes to transport the Chipilin vaccines to China, India, El Salvador, Uruguay, Australia, anywhere you want my man!"

El Cadejo said, "we need to get rid of dirty energy Richie, and I believe we can do it through the Cherry Club and Pfizer." Branson nodded his head in agreement. El Cadejo told Branson if he would agree to coordinate the distribution of the Chipilin vaccine; that he would nominate him for the People for the Ethical Treatment of Animals (PETA) Humanitarian of the Year Award. Branson said, "you can count on me."

The People for the Ethical Treatment of Animals (PETA) admired El Cadejo and the president of PETA decided to name the PETA Humanitarian of the Year Award – the PETA EL CADEJO AWARD.

They knew that El Cadejo could help them with the elimination of the savage hunting expeditions and trophy awards of animals. They were sick and tired of ignorant foreign hunters that would fly to South Africa and other African countries just to hunt and shoot elephants, lions, and other so-called animals.

Given an award to Branson would bring more awareness to hunting practices where the head of the animal is made into a trophy. Simply, for the human satisfaction of shooting wild animals and deciding to show off to their friends how valiant and courageous they have been to shoot animals. Have you ever seen an animal use weapons to shoot other animals or humans? No. They are more advanced than the stupidity of humans who have developed ignorant sports such as hunting to fulfill one's pride and ego. To place the heads of animals that they shot on their walls. For what?

The PETA event was held at the Biltmore Hotel in Downtown Los Angeles and the leaders of PETA demanded that only vegetarian food be served. Especially since Branson is a strong vegetarian who does not believe in eating animal meats.

The event was magnificent. El Cadejo wore a beautiful tuxedo and was designated to give the award to Mr. Branson. This was the opportunity that El Cadejo had been waiting for – to make a public announcement regarding the El Chipilin vaccine.

Of course, the event required social distancing of six feet, and everyone was required to wear masks. PETA knew the hustle and sold each mask with the logo of PETA on it for $5. Fuck, they even sold T-shirts and hats at the event with the PETA logo. The T-shirts went for $20 and the hats went for $30. When a guest asked, "why so expensive?" one of the PETA volunteers flipped and went ghetto. "Motherfucker, we have single mothers making T-shirts, hats, and doing hand embroidered logs and designs. We pay them $15 per hour. So why the fuck would a $30 hat be too much? You cheap motherfucker!" The snob guest felt embarrassed and said to the PETA volunteer, "I will take one of each: a mask, a T-shirt, and a hat." The PETA volunteer said "that is $55 you little bitch! And you're lucky that you are only paying $55 for organic cotton and handmade masks, shirts, and hats. Made in the USA."

PETA made a killing at the event. An estimated 500 people attended. Around 400 people bought the special package of the mask, T-shirt, and hat. They raked in $22,000 just in merchandise. Plus, Branson gave a $100 million donation. They were set to do advocacy work for the next ten years, unless they would make a mistake of hiring vultures and money hungry administrators who would blow the donation on their salaries, junket trips, and the magical disappearance of funds. Inevitably claiming within two years, "we are broke, and we need more donations to pay the accountants." Typical fundraising strategy.

The cheap attendees that did not buy any merchandise are the Anti-Mask Coalition. They feel that they were born special since their parents and schools would give them Certificates of Achievement and Trophies for simply showing up to school; for yawning, and for playing tether ball and kickball. Some of these individuals would usually win the tether ball, handball, and kickball matches – and the teachers would say "look at Johnny, he excels and he is special." And once he would get home his mom would bake cupcakes for such a grandiose achievement. Little Johnny grew up with a sense of entitlement and anytime he did not want to do something he would simply say "fuck that shit." Little Johnnies grew up and bought big polluting cars to make for the lack of a big dick length. They needed to psychologically and subliminally state "I have a big fucking car, so therefore, I must have a big dick."

When the Governor of California and the Mayor recommended for the Little Johnnies of the world to wear masks due to the pandemic of COVID-19, they would shout in unison "FUCK THAT SHIT!"

El Cadejo was ecstatic. He had achieved his goal: he now had Richard Branson in his back pocket. The devious motherfucker Cadejo.

However, since he had lost some of his magical, supernatural powers, he sometimes would suffer from Borderline Personality Disorder. He met more than five traits out of nine to be officially diagnosed with BPD:

- Fear of abandonment. (People with BPD are often terrified of being abandoned or left alone).

- Unstable relationships

- Unclear or shifting self-image

- Impulsive, self-destructive behaviors

- Self-harm

- Extreme emotional swings

- Chronic feelings of emptiness

- Explosive anger

- Feeling suspicious or out of touch with reality

El Cadejo was abandoned by La Siguanaba, El Cipitio, and El Duende. His own family disowned him due to his evil nature. He could not maintain any stable relationships because he was a perro caliente. He had an unclear, shifting self-image – and would be confused whether he was Black or White. He was led by his evil, greedy, selfish, and self-serving impulses that led to destructive behaviors such as habitual alcoholism and extreme drug use. He loved harming others and harming himself. To the point that he had carved 666 on his body. The sign of the Devil. He was happy one moment and the next he was furious. His mood swings were terrible. He would be laughing one minute and the next minute he would be crying like a little bitch. No matter how much money and material possessions he held through crooked deals from the El Chipilin vaccine, Cherry Club extortion non-profit racket, and Pfizer vaccine scam, he always felt empty. If he did not get his way, he would explode into an uncontrollable fury that led to torture and murder. He was always suspicious of people around him and sometimes he felt that he was in a state of surrealism. The fucker was truly out of touch with reality. When millions were dying due to the COVID-19 virus, he went golfing! What a fucker!

El Cadejo's God was money. Money. Money. Money. Dollars. Dollars. Dollars. He did not give a fuck about humanity. All he cared about was surpassing Jeff Bezos as the wealthiest person in the world. He wanted to become not just a trillionaire, but the most powerful motherfucker in the world.

He wanted to take revenge of El Cipitio, former U.S. president and La Siguanaba reigning Pope of the Catholic Church.

How could he achieve it? Well, by continuing to be the CEO of the *Cherry Club* and Chair of the Board for *Pfizer.* The stock investments for the El Chipilin vaccine would become more expensive and powerful than Amazon, Apple, Microsoft, Coca-Cola, and all the other powerful brands and corporations throughout the world.

He just needed to reach out to someone who could make the El Chipilin vaccine work properly. He knew that COVID-19 was going to mutate into various viruses. He needed someone who was familiar with the other killer viruses, who knew organic chemistry, biology, natural cures; an expert in plants, and knowledge of mixing ingredients that could be approved by the U.S. Federal Drug Administration (FDA). He took some sleeping pills so that he could relax and think of someone who would be the perfect high achieving, nerd genius. Who?

El Cadejo went into a deep sleep and in his dreams, he had a vision of Rasputin and El Duende. Grigori Rasputin spoke to him and said, "search, find, and convince your son to help you with the El Chipilin vaccine."

When he woke up at 5:00 a.m. he had his answer: El Duende was the one that could develop a reliable vaccine! He decided to blast The Killer's *Read My Mind* song and started dancing like Elvis Presley.

El Duende had the intellect and medical training since he did his residency at the Mayo Clinic focusing on applied research in finding cures/vaccines for various viruses. He just had to figure a way to finesse his estranged son.

El Cadejo knew how to cajole people and this would have to be extra special. He knew that his son was a little lefty softy. He had been a guerrilla fighter in El Salvador, and he admired El Che Guevara tremendously.

El Cadejo knew exactly what kind of gift he could give to his leftist son. El Cadejo had the actual jar with the hands of El Che. El Cadejo had actually served as an advisor to the CIA and Bolivian government in searching and finding the exact location of El Che Guevara when he was trying to instill an uprising/insurrection among the campesino in Bolivia. What El Che did not realize was that the peasants were not interested in joining a revolution and that he would be betrayed by one of his own followers. El Cadejo was present when El Che was shot to death and the Bolivian General ordered for his hands to be chopped off since they were afraid that he possibly returned from death – to avenge. Therefore, they took precautions by chopping his two hands off. El Cadejo was the actual soldier who committed the cutting of the hands and he kept them as trophies. He knew that El Duende would feel honored to have the actual hands of El Che Guevara, his revolutionary hero, who was actually becoming a doctor. When in the process, El Che decided to become an armed guerrilla with Fidel Castro in Cuba. Even though El Che was originally from Argentina. Hence, the nickname, El Che.

El Che also had a secret gift that he wanted to entice his son with, but he would reveal it once El Duende would agree to meet with him.

El Cadejo decided to send El Duende a WhatsApp message. He sent him The Cranberries song *Linger* via a YouTube video. He knew that El Duende had inherited some of his cold-blooded criminal genetics. But he had a softy side and he loved The Cranberries. El Duende also inherited some of the Borderline Personality Disorders from his evil father: El Cadejo. Especially the one where he felt an infinite sense of abandonment and loneliness since his mother and father had neglected him and his twin brother: El Cipitio.

Once El Duende received El Cadejo's WhatsApp message, he began to cry. Like a little pussy. Once he heard *Linger,* it broke his heart. Then, to add more melancholy the manipulative Cadejo sent him Juan Gabriel's *Yo No Se Que Me Paso* and his all-time favorite, Alvaro Torres' *Nada Se Compara.*

El Duende could not resist. He texted a message back and wanted to come across via his gangster roots. "What the fuck you want motherfucker?"

El Cadejo smiled from here to the moon. He knew that the songs would work! They usually worked in manipulating La Siguanaba. Especially when he would dedicate Los Bukis *Que Mala* to her.

El Cadejo sent a second text requesting to meet at the local Costco food court. He wanted to buy a vanilla ice cream and a hot dog. El Duende simply replied and said yes. He loved hot dogs with lots of relish, mustard, and ketchup.

They agreed on the date and time. El Cadejo arrived early since he had to get a membership card in order to be able to buy food. El Duende arrived on his motorcycle.

El Cadejo could not believe it. El Duende was also in disbelief that the evil fucker had survived the hit they put on him.

Like they say "la sangre llama." They did a fist bump and told each other – "keep your social distance."

El Cadejo got the hot dogs and vanilla ice cream. He

gave one of each to El Duende who said, "these are best fucking hot dogs in the world!" and they both laughed.

El Cadejo cut through the bullshit and got to business right away. He told El Duende that he had the IQ and the medical training that he received at the Mayo Clinic in Rochester, Minnesota to be able to develop the vaccine to cure and counter the effects of COVID-19; but that he had the secret ingredient.

El Duende asked "what is the secret ingredient?" and El Cadejo "pues, El Chipilin." El Duende told El Cadejo that he would do it if he gets a billion-dollar advance and 10% of the vaccine profits, de por vida.

El Cadejo told his son, "You inherited my sophisticated negotiating skills. I like it and you got it my boy! Un billon de dolares is cool. We got CBP 13 collecting taxes from all the gangs throughout the United States. A billion bolas is chump change for real gangsters."

El Cadejo and El Duende did the gangster handshake and the deal was sealed. Before they parted ways El Cadejo wanted to give the secret ingredients that he had obtained from El Brujo principal from Izalco de El Salvador. El Cadejo wrote the secret ingredients on a napkin for El Duende: the indigenous vaccine against COVID-19, consisting of a mixture of garlic, red onion, cola de caballo, limes, oranges, and ginger.

El Duende could not escape his gangster background and told his deadbeat, loser father "orale homes. VENMO me the $1 billion today if you want me to create the vaccine, me entiendes mendez? Si no, the deal is off, ese."

"No worries Little Duende, I got your back little vato. I'm gonna send you the $1 billion through el pinche VENMO. Orale, ese," said El Cadejo.

El Duende had to get to work. He texted Mayo Clinic's CEO Gianrico Farrugia, M.D. to ask him if he could use the laboratories and high-tech equipment at the Rochester headquarters to work on the development of the COVID-19 vaccine. Dr. Farrugia, said "o.k. but if you are successful in developing the vaccine, with a 50% success rate or more, you will have to agree to donate $10 billion to the Mayo Clinic for future research and to provide scholarships for future doctors. Is that a deal amigo?" El Duende responded via Messenger and simply wrote "Si, the El Duende Foundation would be truly honored to help the Mayo Clinic. You just have to treat me to a spumoni ice cream once I develop the vaccine."

El Duende got to work. He even moved to The Kahler Grand Hotel. He needed privacy, his own space, and a place where he could relax when not in the laboratory developing one of the world's most important vaccines in the world.

He did not want what occurred from 1918 to 1920. The deaths of between 50 to 100 million human beings due to the Spanish Flu (The Blue Death). Why was it called The Blue Death? The skin color and body of infected individuals would turn bluish once they were about to die or once dead. Hence, The Blue Death.

El Duende worked day and night at the Mayo Clinic laboratory. He even ordered an inflatable bed to sleep there when he was too exhausted to return to the hotel.

He would personally take Tylenol, Zinc, and Vitamin D pills as preventative care. He wanted to prepare his body to avoid becoming infected by COVID-19.

All of a sudden, a lightning bolt idea hit El Duende. Why not simply mix garlic, red onion, cola de caballo, limes, oranges, ginger, El Chipilin, Tylenol, Zinc, and Vitamin D?

He began to feel extreme heart palpitations. He could not believe that he potentially may have thought of the vaccine against COVID-19. He knew that his secret hero, Dr. James Watson, would be truly proud of him. El Duende just happened to have been one of the best students that Dr. Watson had. He learned a great deal from the Nobel Prize winner since he discovered The Double Helix (the structure of DNA). Except that he was embarrassed by the fact that Dr. Watson had consistently made racist and sexist comments. El Duende was particularly embarrassed when Dr. Watson gave a lecture at UC Berkeley where he stated "Whenever you interview fat people, you feel bad, because you know you're not going to hire them". Dr. Watson was an equal opportunity offender. He was anti-fat.

Another big influence of El Duende's intellect is Joseph Graves, Jr. who he followed closely and was one of his favorite guests on PBS television where Mr. Grave shared the following example:

"A few years ago, during the census, a census worker came to my house and wanted to take data about the racial composition of the people who lived there. I opened the door and she asked me, "Well, you know, how do you describe yourself racially?" And I looked at the form and said, "Well, based upon the form you have here, the best thing that I would be described as is African American, or black." And so, she clicked the "black" box, and then asked me, "Well, how many other people live here?" I said, "My wife and our two children."

So, she immediately went in to block in "black" for my wife and children. I said, "No, you didn't ask me what my wife's ethnicity was." And at that point, she took two steps back from the door and asked me, "Well, what would you describe your wife as?" And I said, "Looking at the categories, you don't really have a category for my wife here. She's Korean, and based upon what you have here, Asian is the best guess."

And she then asked, "Well, how would you describe your kids?" as she was about to check the "black" category. And I told her, "Well, you just asked me what my wife was and I told you she was Korean, so how do you come to the conclusion that my kids are black?" At that point, she took another step back from the door. And I said, "Well, based upon the categories you have, you're going to have to describe my kids as other."

And the "other" category sort of describes what we go through on a daily basis. When the children are with my wife, people think that they're Asian. Both my sons play piano, and when they're in piano recitals, people think that they're Asian. However, when they're in sports and with me, playing basketball, they talk about my son's natural athletic ability, and they think he's black.

So here you have children who have a mixed ancestry

who are racially defined by which parent they're seen with and which activity they're involved in, which match the stereotypical views of people about what racial groups are supposed to do."

Simply, El Duende was on a path to save humanity. He knew that his competitors included the following big pharma corporations: Moderna, MRNA, Oxford Astra Zeneca, Novavax, Sanofi, and Pfizer BNT 1620 MRNA.

He did something that was unprecedented. He prayed. He prayed and prayed. He asked his mother, Pope Siguanaba, for wisdom and guidance in his journey to create the vaccine that would save humanity. He texted El Cipitio to get some optimism and El Cipitio texted back "You got this bro!"

He spent months and months converting the natural plants and ingredients into chemicals. He finally was successful in mixing just the right ingredients. He finally had a vaccine to find COVID-19 and to destroy it. However, he discovered that it was only 50% effective since COVID-19 was like a monster that would develop into different virus strands. He had to find a vaccine that would truly eliminate COVID-19. He lost 10 *lbs* due to the strenuous work and intense pressure. Similar to Greta Thunberg's intensity. Speaking of Greta. She heard about El Duende through a Google search. She was astounded. A ten-year old, three and a half foot tall, little fucking genius environmentalist. She had to call him via Skype or even ZOOM.

Greta finally found someone that she could relate to and she actually found El Duendito attractive. She first started following El Duende on Instagram and she sent him a message that she wanted to speak to him via video conferencing.

El Duende ignored her messages, since his number one goal was to find the vaccine against COVID-19. He was competing against China, India, and Russia.

He was so fucking annoyed to hear the little bell on his smartphone. The cheap fucker had a SAMSUNG Galaxy S9 and he did not want to upgrade to a 5G cell phone since these types of phones help to spread Coronavirus – since they were initially produced in China, and the factory workers purposely coughed on the inside wiring of the 5G cell phones to spread COVID-19 through the wavelengths produced by the phones.

Mysteriously, El Duende received a photo of Pupusa and Flor de Izote.

He could not resist. He clicked on the Pupusa photo. It was Greta. El Duende could not believe it. She had linked a message which stated "I want to speak to you El Duende. I will call you via ZOOM from Sweden tomorrow at 10:00 a.m. U.S. Midwestern Time. Answer the call.

El Duende started to crack up. He literally had to take sleeping pills, since his adrenaline was running on 200 miles per hour. He had to get the vaccine completed.

He went to sleep early at 11:00 p.m. to be awake for the ZOOM call from Greta. She called at 9:59 a.m. and he answered. She asked him, "would you like to speak in English or Spanish?" El Duende said, "We can speak in English cipota." Greta started to giggle.

She got down to business. She said that she had done

Google research on COVID-19 and the culture and vegetation of El Salvador. "I have made a major discovery," she shared. "I viewed a video of how peasants in the small villages of El Salvador grow and then cook Flore de Izote. Guess what? Those households do not get infected by COVID-19! Do you know what that means chiquito Duendito?"

El Duende almost had a heart attack. He replied, "What the fuck? You mean to tell me that you have discovered the natural plant to fight off COVID-19 – and it's none other than La Flor de Izote?"

"Yes," said Greta with her exquisite Swedish accent. "A la gran puta!" shouted El Duende. Greta had ordered a Flor de Izote to be delivered via DHL from El Salvador to Sweden. She Googled how to cook Flor de Izote from El Salvador. She was impressed with the simplicity of the cooking process. She prepared the Flor de Izote for her father and herself, since both had been identified positive with COVID-19. They ate the Flor de Izote con huevos revueltos. The next morning, they woke up completely healthy and they both decided to call a doctor to come and conduct a new COVID-19 test for both. It was amazing, they both tested negative! Greta was in awe and she shared with El Duende that she needed to reach him and to meet him in person to tell him the wonderful news.

Greta told El Duende, "I've been stuck in my apartment in Sweden since COVID-19 began. The least that you can do is to come visit me. Please bring me organic Pupusas. And I would like to watch Titanic with you. I love Leonardo DiCaprio and I know that his favorite food are Pupusas. Remember, you will have to bring a Fitted N95 mask in order for us to be safe while we watch Titanic on Netflix. Duende, is it a deal?"

El Duende said, "Yes, I will take a box of N95 and surgical masks for us, I will take Pupusas, and I will make sure to wash my hands with bacteria killing soap. The least I can do for you is to take some Pupusas de Loroco, since you have discovered the natural cure against COVID-19: La Flor de Izote. I will also take some Sopa de Chipilin. We have to keep this a major secret and we have to submit it to the World Health Organization for approval, before Trump cuts a deal with McKesson Corporation for vaccine exclusivity and distribution."

Then, El Duende had an *aha* moment. He might as well just email Jeff Bezos, the founder of Amazon, to set up a breakfast meeting. He wanted to propose to Jeff if Amazon would agree to be the distributor of El Chipilin and Flore de Izote vaccines.

He knew Jeff Bezo's secret. As a child, Jeff wanted to be Captain Kirk from Star Trek and that he would also settle for being Spock. Therefore, El Duende decided to comb his hair exactly like Captain Kirk. He wore a light blue shirt just like Spock's and he even wore Vulcan ears!

They met at the San Juan Capistrano Mission, since El Duende loved to visit the California Missions in order to admire the architecture and hard work of the indigenous – who actually built the Missions. Once El Duende arrived, he saluted Jeff Bezos with the Vulcan hand signal, inside the San Juan Capistrano Chapel. Where Father Junipero Serra gave mass.

Once El Duende greeted Jeff with the Vulcan hand signal, no more was needed to be said to Jeff. He was sold. He told El Duende right off the bat, "yes, Amazon will distribute your vaccines. We need to save lives immediately. Of course, you have to give 10% of every sale to me." El Duende replied, "No hay pedo homes, 10%, done deal."

El Duende was curious as to why Jeff wanted to also meet at Orange County's San Juan Capistrano. Jeff said, "well, I'm looking to expand more distribution centers and I figured that San Juan Capistrano would be a great city for us to build our next warehouse – to distribute more products, especially your vaccine, in the OC."

Jeff agreed that he would send a one-page contract to be reviewed and signed by El Duende.

During the private meeting with Jeff, El Duende opened up and told him that he understood why he wanted to be the wealthiest man alive. His father was not present. He was raised by a Cuban immigrant stepfather. El Duende said, "you want to impress your real father so that he will accept you. I understand the conflict. I myself detest my evil father, who is not accepted either by Whites or Blacks, since he is biracial."

El Duende revealed El Cadejo's ultimate secret and true nature. He was similar to Spock – half Vulcan and half human. El Cadejo was half good and half evil. He was confused and full of fury. His deepest secret was that he loved to cross dress at night. He would even put on lingerie that he would buy from Victoria's Secret.

El Duende committed the ultimate sin of sharing that humiliating secret of El Cadejo. He was a cross dresser.

Now, if El Cadejo were to find out, El Duende's life would be over. El Cadejo would have to murder his own son.

The irony of it all, was that El Duende did not realize why his father, El Cadejo, hated him with a passion. Sooner or later, the truth is always revealed. And El Duende was about to find out that it did not matter that he was about to become a trillionaire through the COVID-19 vaccines of El Chipilin and La Flor de Izote. He had found love with Greta.

What El Duende and Jeff Bezos did not realize was that the Supreme Leader of North Korea, Kim Jong Un, had paid his top spies to record their conversation and meeting at the San Juan Capistrano Mission. The spies simply hacked Jeff Bezos and El Duende's cheap ass cell phones. The North Korean spies remotely turned on the microphones within Bezo's Apple phone and El Duende's SAMSUNG 4G Network.

Now, Kim Jong Un had the perfect excuse to blackmail El Cadejo. He had made an executive order for all dogs to be caught and be banned from North Korea. He felt that the dogs were spreading world viruses and plagues. He also had a grand plan for the millions of dogs to be trapped in North Korea, to be slain, skinned, and for the meat to be frozen and packaged. For it to be used to feed his hungry and starving population. Of course, he would not tell the North Koreans that he would ultimately feed them dog meat.

Kim Jong Un would also make a trade-off with El Cadejo. The Supreme Leader would provide El Cadejo with El Duende's revelation of his cross-dressing and of his biracial secret. In return, the Supreme Leader would request for El Cadejo to steal the vaccines from El Duende and to provide billions of free vaccines to North Korea. This would help make the Supreme Leader not just a God within his own country, but throughout the world. He would be able to manipulate and blackmail other world leaders if he had access to the ultimate COVID-19 vaccines: El Chipilin and La Flor de Izote.

The Supreme Leader requested for El Cadejo to meet with him in Pyongyang since he wanted to host El Cadejo as royalty. He would treat El Cadejo to view a rerun of a classic Chicago Bulls game that included Dennis Rodman. He also made a special request from El Cadejo, to bring him a Combo #1 from IN-N-OUT BURGER. With a Coke and onions. That food was Kim Jong Un's favorite when he was an undercover middle school, chubby student at Rosemont Middle School in La Crescenta, California. He never forgot those American days. That is where he became a basketball fan and an IN-N-OUT regular. After playing basketball, he loved going to IN-N-OUT to get the little white cups filled with fresh ketchup. He loved sipping and licking the ketchup left at the bottom of the little paper cups.

Now, finally decades later, he would once again have an IN-N-OUT burger. He also requested ten little white cups filled up with fresh ketchup. He was not able to sleep thinking about how he would eat the big ass burger, filled with cheese, onions, tomatoes, that secret sauce. He also asked El Cadejo to freeze his soda that comes with the combo. He demanded that it be regular Coca-Cola. "None of that Diet shit," he wrote in his secret messages sent to El Cadejo, through his top North Korean spies.

El Cadejo arrived with two #1 IN-N-OUT combos. One

for the Supreme Leader and the other for his sister: Kim Yo-jong. A black belt in various martial arts and a fan of mixed martial arts.

He was greeted better than when Donald Trump met with Kim Jong Un in North Korea's demilitarized zone. Trump had the balls to cross the 1953 armistice line separating North Korea and South Korea. But Trump did not have the COVID-19 vaccine, while El Cadejo did have it.

El Cadejo was picked up at the armistice line and driven in a private, white limousine to the Supreme Leader's private home. Built underground.

Kim Jong Un eagerly awaited the private visit from El Cadejo. El Cadejo was carrying two briefcases: one with the two IN-N-OUT combos and the other carried the El Chipilin and La Flor de Izote COVID-19 vaccines.

The Supreme Leader began eating the triple meat burger immediately. He also simultaneously would suck on the little white cups filled with ketchup. He was back in La Crescenta – and would remember his wild nights of visiting the IN-N-OUTS located in Glendale and Burbank. He hugged El Cadejo and a tear dropped down his cheek. The fucking onions were powerful!

Kim Jong Un said "let's get to business. You kept your side of the bargain and now I have the secret recording from the meeting of El Duende with Jeff Bezos." El Cadejo handed over the briefcases with the vaccines and El Duende handed him the copy of the recording that was placed in a special device that could be hooked up to almost any cell phone to listen to the recording.

El Cadejo was salivating to hear the secret recording. Kim Jong Un and El Cadejo kept social distance of six feet. He began to listen, and he heard the conversation; and once he began to listen to the terrifying part – he began to shake out of nervousness and fury. He heard El Duende telling Jeff Bezos the following "El Cadejo is biracial and he is a crossdresser at night."

El Cadejo began to howl. Howl so loud that almost everyone in North Korea could hear his evil howl. His eyes turned bright red. Even The Supreme Leader was astounded and taken aback with extreme fear. He finally realized that he literally had invited *the devil* into his home.

El Cadejo could not withstand the fury. He quietly muttered the following profound words "I will torture, murder, and I will eat El Duende. He is dead to me. He is not my son. How can he be my son if I am Black and he came out White? I detest Whites!!!

The Supreme Leader and his bodyguards began to see El Cadejo transform into a mixture of Black and White. He transformed into the evilest looking dog/wolf. His teeth were razor sharp and his body was extraordinarily huge and muscular. The claws from his feet were extraordinarily huge. His testicles were bigger than an elephant's balls.

Kim Jong Un became so intimidated, that he began to drink his Coca-Cola with no straw. His bodyguards could not hurt nor kill The Son of the Prince of Darkness: EL CADEJO.

One of El Cadejo's secret weapon was his urine. He would purposely inject himself with the COVID-19 virus or any other virus/disease to contaminate his enemies (or target) and he would purposely piss on them to infect them.

That was his plan. He was going to miar (piss on) El Duende!

He told the Supreme Leader "Me tengo que ir a la mierda. Nos vemos cerote dictador."

The Supreme Leader was speechless. His translator told him what El Cadejo said to him before leaving. Of course, he translated differently by saying "Enjoy your French fries, little chubby Teletubby." The Supreme Leader started to crack up uncontrollably and started dancing the Elmo *Happy Dance*. He loved the Muppets.

A few days later, The Supreme Leader fell into a deep coma. The fucker, El Cadejo, had purposely pissed on his burger.

Getting back to the little fucker, El Duende.

He loved visiting Sweden since he got to hang out with Greta. He began to develop a crush on her since she reminded him of *Heidi, Girl of the Alps* cartoon that he would assiduously watch in El Salvador.

One day, he even had a Freudian slip and called Greta, *Heidi*. She was pissed and gave him the deadly stare. Of course, El Duende was slick and he gave her a *peperecha* so that she would regain her composure and be loving once again. Of course, they kept it real by staying six feet apart. Once they were getting all lovey-dovey, El Cadejo had to fuck it up. The fucker texted El Duende, in the middle of his Karaoke singing of Luis Miguel's *Te Quiero* song.

El Cadejo was gonna go gangster on his own son. El Cadejo began the call "wat up *ese*?" El Duende was shocked that his bitch ass dad was referring to him as *ese*. El Duende was coldhearted and said "don't call me *ese*, homie. I don't bang anymore. I am heading to be the first light skinned indigenous trillionaire of the world. Call me, Mr. Duende."

El Cadejo growled and decided to become the deceiving Cadejo – just like the Devil – when he tricked Adam and Eve by speaking through a snake. He seduced both of them to eat the forbidden fruit.

El Cadejo told El Duende to meet with him. El Duende responded by saying "I will think about it. I am busy right now. I will text you when I have more time and when I am ready to meet."

In the meantime, El Duende began to implement his distribution system with Amazon. Jeff Bezos opened new distribution centers/warehouses throughout the world. He needed to double, and possibly, triple his capacity. He hired millions of new workers at $15 per hour, in any country, with the possibility of promotions and pay increases.

El Duende had requested that he be a benevolent leader when it came to the distribution of the COVID-19 vaccines. El Duende also, set the price of each COVID-19 vaccine to be at $20. He said "what is a life to save worth? $20 is a pretty good deal, with no taxes or shipping costs." El Duende's foundation decided to cover the tax fees and shipping and handling costs.

Vladimir Putin from Russia, and other world leaders, requested private meetings with El Duende. They wanted to get El Chipilin and Flor de Izote vaccines to fight COVID-19 and other viruses/diseases.

Jeff Bezos even took on the persona of Captain Kirk and started to tell his leadership team "full speed ahead." And also, he would paraphrase Spock by saying, "the needs of the many are great. We need to get the vaccine to everyone."

50 to 100 million new employees were hired throughout the world to manage the distribution centers and to drive the trucks and manage the drones to deliver the vaccines to remote villages.

Word started spreading that El Duende and Greta had discovered the magic to cure and fight COVID-19.

They began to become household names. Children began to get the vaccine through Amazon; and the families were forever grateful. People in India would tell the drivers to please tell El Duende and Greta thank you. That they were truly heroes.

People began writing letters, emails, and posted on social media how El Duende's hard work at the Mayo Clinic laboratories had paid off in creating the COVID-19 vaccine. Some would also give credit to Greta for discovering the natural curing powers of the Flor de Izote. Of course, since she was female, many of the patriarchal, machista societies would refuse to recognize her contributions. Therefore, El Duende took all of the credit. This was reflective of other scientific, artistic, and political achievements. The women, sometimes, were the ones making amazing discoveries in science, or painting amazing big-eyed children or led initial organizing efforts in creating amazing social movements.

Greta was well aware of this and she told El Duende "you don't believe?" Then, she began to further educate El Duende about Henrietta Lacks, Fannie Lou Hamer, Shirley Chisholm, Margaret Keane, and Mary Moreno.

El Duende asked "Who the fuck were they?" Henrietta Lacks was a Black woman whose cells were stolen without her consent and many medical cures have been achieved from the billions of cells that came from her. Fannie Lou Hamer was a strong lady who fought in the South for Civil Rights. She worked the lands and was an inspiration to thousands of people that she helped to organize and empower. Shirley Chisholm was the first Black female U.S. presidential candidate in the 1970s. Margaret Keane painted amazing portraits of children with huge eyes, amazing art talent. But her husband used to pretend to the world that he had painted them, when in fact, Margaret Keane was the artist. Maria Moreno began organizing farm works in California in the 1950s and 1960s before Cesar Chavez's United Farm Workers (UFW). How about Hedy Lamarr, a world-famous beautiful actress who was an inventor. She came up with the idea and patented amazing technology but was never given proper credit nor paid for her amazing invention that she patented through: https://patents.google.com/patent/US2292387.

El Duende was blown away once Greta schooled him on the history of women who were not given proper credit for their amazing contributions in improving our world. The same thing was happening to Greta, but she did not give a fuck. She was already well known worldwide and could stand her ground.

She was truly an independent woman. El Duende was simply lucky that she developed a crush on his little ass.

El Duende was becoming even more popular that El Cipitio and La Siguanaba. People began to place his portrait on their walls and on their Facebook and Instagram pages/posts.

Some even began to place his tiny portrait on their necklaces made by Roberto Coin. Even Roberto Coin wanted to meet and hang out with El Duende. He was overwhelmed with the adulation and love. Finally, his heart was being filled with positivity and he felt that void of loneliness was being repaired. He always longed for his father's and mother's love. He was a neglected child.

He began to do introspection and began to realize that he was seeking affirmation and love. And that finally, through his amazing IQ and intellectual level, he was able to develop a worldwide known and needed vaccine against COVID-19.

60 Minutes and *Aqui y Ahora* from Univision, decided to do special exclusive stories about El Duende. They were shocked that they had not really heard of the little vato.

The producers looked into his background and were shocked that he came from a little village in El Salvador. That he would play freely in nature and lived off the fruits and vegetables that were grown by the campesinos. He himself was a campesino who lived in a little shack. They could not understand how a person who came from such poverty, could be so intelligent to have developed the vaccine against COVID-19. The producers of *60 Minutes* started to insinuate that El Duende had most likely stolen the vaccine from the

Mayo Clinic's renowned doctors and scientists. They even went as far as contacting Dr. Gianrico Farrugia, the president and CEO of the Mayo Clinic. He was shocked that they were questioning the integrity of El Duende.

He was pissed off since he had not had his daily Espresso coffee. He told *60 Minutes* "Look fuckers, just because he comes from a poverty-stricken background does not mean that he is not intelligent. He is actually the most intelligent human being according to Mensa International. Are you mensos?"

The *60 Minutes* producers had to look up what Mensa was, and they were shocked to discover that El Duende was the unofficial president/leader of Mensa International. An organization that only accepts the smartest human beings in the world and El Duende was the president. Then, they Googled mensos and they were shocked to find it simply means *"dummies."*

They had to beat *Aqui y Ahora* in booking El Duende. They had to be the first to interview and profile the little fucker that discovered the vaccine to COVID-19.

They had the bilingual producer call El Duende, since she had an accent and they assumed that El Duende would also have an accent. The producers wanted to be chummy when she called El Duende. She obtained his cell phone number from Dr. Farrugia. She began the conversation by saying "Hola Guanaco!" and El Duende flipped. He said right away "who the fuck is this? Are you a former chola from 18?" The *60 Minutes* producer cleared her throat and said right away, "no sir, I am calling from *60 Minutes*. That was my friend from the barrio who called you. But it is me that would really like to speak to you, since I graduated from an Ivy League school."

El Duende simply asked "What do you want?" and the producer said "we would like to interview you for *60 Minutes*. We would like to fly you to El Salvador – to visit your humble beginnings and to showcase your amazing trajectory. We would like to make you into an international hero. Are you in Mr. Duende?"

He said "yeah, homegirl. It's all good. You best record my best side of my face for the interview. And I want a professional make-up artist, hair stylist, and professional lighting and audio experts. I don't want no interns doing my profile. You got it Ivy League girl?" She was offended that he used the term *girl,* but she needed the exclusive story and had to give El Duende a pass since she was impressed that a 3 and a half foot tall person could have such brain power.

The producer said, "we will email you all of the details and attachments of paperwork that you need to fill out to give us exclusivity and permission to interview you." El Duende simply said "You got it *girl.*" And to fuck around, he purposely played the Nick Jr. *Girl Power* song just before he hung up. The producer was in shock. She had just spoken to the world's smartest person and he was playing the Nick Jr. *Girl Power* song and he was not being politically correct nor courteous.

Bill Owens, the executive producer, was elated once the intern producer told him that she had secured El Duende.

Owens called an executive team meeting. He said that

this would be one of the most important profile interviews ever to be done by *60 Minutes;* and that no limit on resources would exist. He said that George Soros, Michael Bloomberg, Francoise Bettencourt Meyers, and Jacqueline Mars were personally interested in the upcoming profile. And each had agreed to donate for the costs and production of the special episode. Jacqueline Mars had even agreed to provide a year of free chocolate candies to all of the *60 Minutes* staff for one year. The entire staff burst into applause and they gasped with amazement of such generosity.

First, they would profile the small village where El Duende grew up. They would interview people who knew him as a child, and they would interview Joaquin Villalobos since he had trained El Duende to become a deadly commando urbano during the Salvadoran Civil War. They would also send producers and private investigators to also seek out any secrets they would find in relation to El Duende. They had to go to the ghettos and prisons, where some of the gangster friends of El Duende resided. They had to interview Mexican Mafia leaders who were originally from 18 Street and had done drive-by shootings and graffiti paintings with El Duende.

One of the major findings from one of the undercover private investigators, was that El Duende was nicknamed El Ch'orti' by the Disiocheros. He was the shortest in stature yet obtained the highest level of leadership within 18 Street and he was the first Salvi that was admitted to be a full-fledged carnal (or high ranking member) of the *Mexican Mafia.* However, in his clean-cut intellectual persona, he was known as El Duende.

He was not just called El Ch'orti' due to his height, but that he came from the indigenous Mayan Tribe known as Los Ch'orti's in El Salvador, Honduras, and Guatemala. But El Duende had hidden his indigenous roots since he came out chelito or guerito. Light skinned – to the point of even being confused as a possible Aryan Brotherhood (AB) or a Proud Boy member.

60 Minutes has pretty much broken down his story of being similar to Charlie Chaplin. He came from extreme poverty, had a mother that was not stable, but was amazingly talented and driven. And El Duende, just so happened to have a higher IQ than Albert Einstein. He was born with the gift of having a huge part of his brain with a massive grey matter.

He was a natural when it came to science and math. He knew biology, anatomy, physics, calculus, quantum physics, at a PhD level. There was no limit to his brain power; and *60 Minutes* would focus on his amazing intellectual abilities and showcase El Duende working at the Mayo Clinic laboratory, developing the vaccine for COVID-19. With never before seen footage from his own smartphone video recordings.

They also had to add a shocking piece of news within the episode, to keep the audience watching til' the end. An exclusive one-on-one interview of El Duende, revealing his next big project. The development of a vaccine to cure Racism. Now that would establish *60 Minutes* way ahead of *Aqui y Ahora* with the Nielsen ratings. Who would get to interview El Duende? Lesley Stahl or Bill Whitaker? Owens decided to have both on the story. Stahl would do the El Salvador background story and Bill Whitaker would do the one-on-one with El Duende.

The episode was coming along wonderful. They just needed to get Bill Whitaker and El Duende to do the one-on-one interview at the Mayo Clinic, where El Duende would be showcasing his scientific genius in creating the COVID-19 vaccine and also, his big secret project: to find the cure for racism.

The interview was set up and Bill Whitaker flew with his *60 Minutes* crew to Rochester, Minnesota to meet with El Duende at The Kahler Grand Hotel; and then they would take a stroll to the Mayo Clinic's top secret laboratory chambers.

Whitaker was a little nervous since he knew that El Duende had been a merciless guerrilla killer and a serial killer gangster. However, El Duende had now reformed and he was now a world renowned hero/scientific genius.

The interview began and El Duende decided to wear his laboratory coat with his embroidered name on it: EL DUENDE.

They both sat down and the TV crew had already set up the cameras, lighting, while makeup was done on El Duende.

El Duende looked magnificent. Whitaker began the interview by asking El Duende, "How did you come up with the vaccine for COVID-19?" El Duende responded, "Well, now that I have patented, copyrighted, and trademarked my COVID-19 vaccine, I can tell you Bill. I used two powerful plant ingredients: *Crotalaria longirostrata (El Chipilin)* and *La Flor de Izote*, El Salvador's national flower."

El Duende then got up from his chair and decided to show

Bill Whitaker how he mixed the different chemicals with El Chipilin and La Flor de Izote. Bill could not believe what he was seeing. It was amazing. The visuals for *60 Minutes* were powerful. To conclude, the final question for El Duende, was for him to announce his next big project.

Whitaker asked him "So, Mr. Duende, what is your next project or dream in life?" El Duende replied, "I want to develop a vaccine that will cure the disease of racism in America." Whitaker smiled and said, "Do you really think that is possible?" El Duende did not want to give his true motives and plan. He just smiled and said "well, the least we can do is try!" and the interview concluded with Bill Whitaker and El Duende enjoying a sopa de Chipilin and some Flor de Izote with huevos revueltos.

Whitaker signed off by stating "this is the best damn food I have ever had."

El Duende did not want to share with the world what he was truly working on. It was no vaccine. It was a special deadly poison to inject into his own father, El Cadejo, to murder him.

But he had to pretend that he was working on a benevolent project to not raise any suspicions from El Cadejo. Also, he did not want *People for the Ethical Treatment of Animals* (PETA) to come after his ass.

El Duende kept logging into his JP Morgan Chase bank account. He was counting down the minutes to see when he would officially become a trillionaire.

He stayed up all night with Greta, viewing his profits growing astronomically. He had named his Preferred Business Account: EL CHIPILIN VACCINE, INC.

Once midnight came, he hit the trillion-dollar mark. The Stock Market went bananas. Everyone was investing and buying EL CHIPILIN VACCINE stock. It was pandemonium.

El Duende appeared on every single major newspaper and magazine cover. Forbes magazine titled their cover: *El Duende, Tycoon for the Ages: Mr. Trillionaire.*

To top it off, that same Sunday at 7:00 p.m. *60 Minutes* aired the special profile focused on El Duende. Over 5 billion people tuned in since they wanted to know who discovered and created the El Chipilin COVID 19 Vaccine.

They also wanted to know if they could get it cheaper than $20. To their big surprise, El Duende made an announcement that each vaccine would be sold for $10 for the working class of the world. He became bigger than former president El Cipitio and Pope Siguanaba.

People began to advocate for El Duende to be designated a Saint by not just the Catholic Church but also other religions. He was an international folk hero and a worldwide celebrity.

He had to stay in his suite at the Kahler Grand Hotel since the media wanted to mob him. He became spectacularly famous and wealthy. The wealthiest fucker in the world.

But he still had a deep hole in his heart. He missed his mother and always felt a deep sense of emptiness since he had an absentee father.

While El Duende was busy creating the COVID-19 vaccine, El Cadejo had gone on a rampage. He purposely began fires in Australia, in the United States, Brazil, and many other countries.

El Duende had to put a stop to it. But how could he make

his own father stop being evil? He had to do the unthinkable. He flew to the University of Zurich in Germany and also Yokohama University in Japan. To use their laboratories; and to also visit Urnerboden located in the Swiss canton known as Uri to meet Elias Landolt, a renowned geobotanist who was an expert on Switzerland's native plants/flora. Also, El Duende purchased a NovaSeq 6000 to sequence human, dog, and plant DNA. He wanted to find the DNA sequence of El Cadejo, to be able to develop a combination of chemicals and plants to destroy El Cadejo.

Through the mentorship of Mr. Landolt, El Duende was able to identify azaleas and rhododendrons (flowering plants) that contain toxins that may cause vomiting, diarrhea, coma, and potentially, even death for dogs. The bulbs in tulips and daffodils may cause serious stomach problems, difficulty breathing, and increased heart rate. Eating just a few Sago palm seeds may be enough to cause vomiting, seizures, and key organ failure.

Also, El Duende had a new extremely powerful ally; none other than Kim Yo-jong, the new Leader of North Korea. She wanted revenge since El Cadejo poisoned her brother, Kim Jong-un.

What El Duende and Kim Yo-jong did not realize was El Cadejo's grand plan had begun in North Korea. What he gave to Kim Jong-un were vaccines that had chemicals to destroy human beings.

El Cadejo's ultimate secret plan was to eliminate all humans and for dogs to take over the world. To become the presidents, kings, queens, and leaders.

He had already begun his master plan through the spread of COVID-19 and other diseases. Now, it was up to El Duende, Greta, and Kim Yo-jong to stop El Cadejo's evil plan. Now it made sense to Kim Yo-jong as to why his brother had passed an executive order for all dogs to be captured. He had an intuition that El Cadejo wanted to eliminate humanity but El Cadejo was sneakier and got to The Supreme Leader first – he got him through his weakness: burgers from IN-N-OUT.

El Duende began developing the injection that would ultimately eliminate El Cadejo: azaleas and rhododendrons, bulbs in tulips and daffodils, Sago palm seeds, cashew seeds, antifreeze, chocolate, and one final ingredient that only *The Vatican* had available. Father Gabriele Amorth became known as the exorcist priest – and he developed a potion that would force demons out of bodies that they had invaded – whether humans or dogs. Father Amorth was quoted as saying the following "all eastern religions are based on a false belief in reincarnation" and "practicing yoga is satanic, it leads to evil just like reading Harry Potter."

El Duende flew to the Vatican to meet with his mother, who happened to be Pope Siguanaba. She was happy to see her son and hugged him as a loving mother would. They had both already forgiven each other. She quoted Matthew 10:8 from the bible *"Heal the sick, raise the dead, cleanse those who have leprosy, drive out demons. Freely you have received, freely give."* She also told El Duende that she was genuinely happy to see his success in developing a COVID-19 vaccine and that he needed to watch his back from El Cadejo. She agreed that she would give him a bottle of the secret potion developed by Father Amorth. She said "the Catholic Church never ever shared with anyone this secret potion that includes holy water that can expel any demons from possessed individuals. John the Baptist originally created the potion and Father Amorth was one of the few who had access to the original holy water, and he knew the secret ingredients!"

Pope La Siguanaba said that she would help El Duende to bring El Cadejo to The Vatican. She was using Cambridge Analytica to see what would persuade El Cadejo. She ran his mental illness conditions that included Borderline Personality Disorder (BPD), Bipolar, Schizophrenia, and Multiple Personalities. Cambridge Analytica suggested for Pope La Siguanaba to send an explicit, white lingerie photo of herself. To hack into El Cadejo's sexual perro urges.

She sent him a photo of herself through WhatsApp and she was hotter than Demi Rose, Ashley Graham, and Cardi B!!

Once El Cadejo received her photo, he started salivating and his little pito got hard and solid. His huevos grew full of testosterone.

Pope La Siguanaba wrote an erotic message: "El Cadejo, come visit me at El Vaticano, I would like to relive one of our wild nights. I have been abstinent since I became La Pope/La Papisa que te quiere pisar bien rico."

El Cadejo howled with laughter and cashed his airline mileage to fly through British Airways via The Boeing 747-436 flight. It could fly at over 825 mph and arrive in The Vatican in four to five hours.

He even took some Viagra pills, took some handcuffs, whips, and vanilla whipped cream. He was ready to eat out. Not at McDonalds, but between La Siguanaba's big ass thighs and big gelatina nalgas. Puro perro caliente!!!

El Duende and Pope La Siguanaba had agreed that once El Cadejo was chained up and ready to get whipped by La Siguanaba, since he was a sadomasochistic chucho – she would inject him with the secret potion to expel his evil demons.

Once he arrived, his pito was hard as nails. He had to put a sweater on top of his penis to cover the bulk/la salchicha. El big sausage.

Pope La Siguanaba received him in her secret bunker room. The hump room where wild sex parties were conducted.

El Cadejo could not believe his eyes. Pope La Siguanaba was wearing her best lingerie and his eyes turned bright red. His balls began to quiver with anticipation. He looked like a bull who had been kept away from las vacas. He growled.

La Siguanaba told him that they would go the torture chamber secret room and he followed, asking no questions. She looked exotica. She simply began to dress him into his favorite leather attire, and she demanded that he wear a leather mask to protect each other from COVID-19. He was more than glad to comply. She chained him up and also handcuffed him. He loved getting whipped before engaging in sexual intercourse.

La Siguanaba asked El Cadejo if he had been injected

by the flu vaccine. He said "no." She responded by saying "well, I got a real surprise for you. I have a flu vaccine injection ready for you." She began to whip the shit out of him to the point that he pissed on himself. Then, she asked him, are you ready for the flu injection my dog?" and he howled and said, "fuck yeah." She immediately proceeded to inject his ass. But with the secret potion to conduct a real exorcism.

As soon as she injected him with John the Baptist original Middle Eastern holy water, El Cadejo's pito and heart started to become soft. Thousands of evil spirits began to escape his body. They exited through his mouth, eyes, ears, pito, and even culo. It was an incredible scene. More dramatic than the avocado vomit from Linda Blair's mouth from The Exorcist movie.

La Siguanaba purposely held a mirror to El Cadejo where he had to confront his own selves. He finally realized that he was a conjoined twin, separated at birth – that El Cadejo Blanco and El Cadejo Negro were ONE!!!

Once El Cadejo's body expelled all of the evil demons. Finally, the bright red eyes disappeared, and he was able to mutter "you tricked me Siguanaba." And La Siguanaba cracked up with her wicked laughter and she said "Si, hijo de la gran puta. Now I am officially your owner and you have no extraordinary evil powers. The demons have been expelled, forever! You will now obey all of my orders." El Cadejo whispered, "I am now a Freemason and I am here to help and to protect humans."

Then, El Cadejo began to cry uncontrollably and simply

concluded by saying "Si, lo que Ud ordene Pope Siguanaba. You are now my master." Then, he requested for them to sing Karaoke and to hold each other tight. He requested Roberto Carlos' El Progreso song so that they could sing it together to celebrate his exorcism and new life as the first ever official Vatican dog: El Cadejo Bueno.

They began to sing together; and they both cried and cried and sang at the top of their lungs:

Yo quisiera poder aplacar una fiera terrible
Yo quisiera poder transformar tanta cosa imposible
Yo quisiera decir tantas cosas que pudieran hacerme
*   sentir bien conmigo*
Yo quisiera poder abrazar mi mayor enemigo

Yo quisiera no ver tantas nubes oscuras arriba
Navegar sin encontrar tantas manchas de aceite en los
*   mares*
Y ballenas desapareciendo por falta de escrúpulos
*   comerciales*
Yo quisiera ser civilizado como los animales
Lá, lá, lá, lá...
Yo quisiera ser civilizado como los animales

Yo quisiera no ver tanto verde en la tierra muriendo
Y en las aguas del río los peces desapareciendo
Yo quisiera gritar que ese tal oro negro no es más que un
*   negro veneno*
Ya sabemos que por todo eso vivimos ya menos

Yo no puedo aceptar ciertas cosas que ya no comprendo

El comercio de armas de guerra de muertes viviendo
Yo quisiera hablar de alegría en vez de tristeza mas no
   soy capaz
Yo quisiera ser civilizado como los animales
Lá, lá, lá, lá...
Yo quisiera ser civilizado como los animales
Lá, lá, lá, lá...
Yo quisiera ser civilizado como los animales

La Siguanaba spoke out loud and asked a question directed to the world "in the end, we realized, that *El Cadejo Blanco* and *El Cadejo Negro* is in all of us. It is ultimately up to each individual, to choose to be good or evil. Which El Cadejo do you choose to be?"

She also wanted to share a message with the world by quoting Matthew 7 "Do not judge, or you too will be judged. [2] For in the same way you judge others, you will be judged, and with the measure you use, it will be measured to you."

Once she snapped out of her philosophical and religious trance, La Siguanaba decided to blast ABBA's song *The Winner Takes It All*, while she laid in bed caressing El Cadejo, while he sobbed like a little bitch:

I don't want to talk
About the things we've gone through
Though it's hurting me
Now it's history
I've played all my cards
And that's what you've done too
Nothing more to say
No more ace to play

The winner takes it all
The loser standing small
Beside the victory
That's her destiny

I was in your arms
Thinking I belonged there
I figured it made sense
Building me a fence
Building me a home
Thinking I'd be strong there
But I was a fool
Playing by the rules

The gods may throw a dice
Their minds as cold as ice
And someone way down here
Loses someone dear
The winner takes it all
The loser has to fall
It's simple and it's plain
Why should I complain...